First published in Great Britain in 2007 by Comma Press
3rd Floor, 24 Lever Street, Manchester M1 1DW
www.commapress.co.uk

'It was just, yesterday' was originally published as 'Det var i går bara' in the collection *Brorsan är matt* (Norstedts, 2007). Reproduced by permission. 'Sing me to sleep' was originally published as 'Syng meg i søvn' in the collection *Bikubesong* (Det Norske Samlaget, 1999). Published by agreement with Hagen Agency AS, Oslo. This translation has been published with the financial support of NORLA. 'She was singing' was originally published as 'Elle chantait' in the anthology *Mères et Filles* (Editions le cherche midi, 2004). Published by agreement with Chantal Galtier Roussel Agence Littéraire, Paris. 'Żurek Soup' was originally published as 'Żurek' in the collection *Gra Na Wielu Bebenkach* (Wydawnictwo Ruta, 2001). Published by agreement with Uitgeverij De Geus. 'Fog Island' was first published as 'Sis Adasi' in the collection *Beş Ada* (Can Yayinlari, 1997). Reproduced by permission of the author. 'Calcutta' was first published as 'Calcutta' in the collection *Handy: dreizehn geschichten in alter manier* (Berlin Verlag, 2007). Reproduced by permission. 'The Closeted Pensioner' was first published as 'Ar Pinsean sa Leithreas' in the collection (*An Fear a Phléasc*, Cló Iar-Chonnachta, 1997). Reproduced by permission of the author and Cló Iar-Chonnachta. 'The Water People' was originally published as 'Vatnsfolkið' in the collection *Vatnsfolkið* (Mál og menning, 1997). Reproduced by permission. 'We Did it Because We Had To' was originally published as 'Učinili smo to jer smo morali' in the collection *U što se zaljubljujemo* (Profil International, 2005). Reproduced by permission of the author. Lyrics from 'Heaven Knows I'm Miserable Now', 'Please Please Please Let me Get What I Want,' 'William It Was Really Nothing', 'Sheila Take a Bow', 'Accept Yourself', 'You've Got Everything Now', 'Pretty Girls Make Graves' and 'Bigmouth Strikes Again' (The Smiths, words and music by Morrissey, S. & Marr, J. © 1984-1987.) reproduced by permission of Universal Music Publishing Group and Artemis Muziekuitgeverij B.V. Lyrics from 'Will Never Marry', 'November Spawned a Monster' and 'Trouble Loves Me' (Morrissey, words by Morrissey, S. & music by Langer, C. W., Street, S and Whyte, A. G., respectively © 1990-1997) reproduced by permission of Artemis Muziekuitgeverij B.V.

Copyright © for all stories remains with the authors. Copyright © for all translations remains with the translators.
Copyright © for this selection belongs to Comma Press. All rights reserved.
The moral right of the authors and translators has been asserted.
A CIP catalogue record of this book is available from the British Library
ISBN: 978-1905583133

The publishers gratefully acknowledge assistance from Arts Council England North West, and the following foundations and institutions who have helped with the launch events for this book: the Golsoncott Foundation, the Granada Foundation, Ireland Literature Exchange, NORLA, the Royal Norwegian Embassy and John Rylands University Library, Manchester.

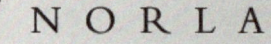

Set in Bembo by XL Publishing Services, Tiverton
Printed and bound in England by SRP Ltd, Exeter.

elsewhere
stories from small town europe

**edited by
maria crossan**

CONTENTS

Introduction	vii
IT WAS JUST, YESTERDAY Mirja Unge Translated by Sarah Death	1
MY CAREER IN GOODNESS Jean Sprackland	11
SING ME TO SLEEP Frode Grytten Translated by Kari Dickson	27
SHE WAS SINGING Danielle Picard Translated by Felicity McNab	47
ŻUREK SOUP Olga Tokarczuk Translated by Antonia Lloyd-Jones	57
FOG ISLAND Mehmet Zaman Saçlıoğlu Translated by Carol Stevens Yürür	71
CALCUTTA Ingo Schulze Translated by John E. Woods	85

CONTENTS

THE CLOSETED PENSIONER   101
Micheál Ó Conghaile
Translated by Gabriel Rosenstock

THE WATER PEOPLE   113
Gyrðir Elíasson
Translated by Vera Juliusdottir

WE DID IT BECAUSE WE HAD TO   119
Roman Simić
Translated by Tomislav Kuzmanović

Contributors   127

Introduction

What do we mean by 'small town'? How and why has this seemingly innocuous demographic term – one up from 'village', a couple down from 'city' – come to function as a pejorative adjective, and as a derogatory description of a particular mindset? Pressed to describe what 'small town' *means*, we could probably reel off a fairly consistent list: narrow- or closed-minded; petty; prejudiced; provincial; parochial. It could perhaps at the same time mean 'twee'; a foolishly overly-idealised space. A small town mindset doesn't and can't look beyond itself; it lacks imagination; it is circumscribed and hemmed in; tied to purely material circumstance; it's a worldview rooted in the past, and looks firmly inward. This apparently innocent delineation of space, free of value judgments in itself, has evolved, jumped categories – from noun phrase to adjective, becoming damning somewhere along the way.

According to a recent estimate, 71 per cent of Europeans currently live outside the continent's 500 largest cities. So, more than two-thirds of us conduct our lives in places indissociable – in language, if not in reality – from these negative connotations. If it is not too lofty an ambition, this anthology has been put together with a view to addressing the lack of complexity in our preconceptions about the small town, its inhabitants and even the stories it generates, and to offer an alternative perspective through the short story.

So what, then, of small town writing? What of literature

INTRODUCTION

taking as its setting, or as its theme, the small town environment? Has this writing suffered the same fate as the term itself; is it perceived as petty, small-minded? Arguably, to some extent it is; it is difficult to put one's finger on a celebratory European 'tradition' of small town literature. In American fiction, small town writing has more of an honourable tradition. It is used as a setting for robust and vivid characters, and is a shorthand for honesty, integrity and hard work; the small town itself offering sanctuary for its inhabitants from the wildernesses beyond. Even the physical device of the small town has been used by writers like Sherwood Anderson to structure collections, following the stories of a particular small town cohort. By contrast the European tradition has tended to view the small town as far less likely to compete – in literary or imaginative terms – with the city, the undisputed centre of all that is metropolitan, cosmopolitan, urbane; all that is *civilised*. In Europe a deep suspicion often marks the literary encounter with the small town; tellingly, one genre that exploits this environment well is crime writing, closely followed by horror, suggesting that the small town in literature functions firmly outside that which is considered desirable. This move from simple noun phrase to loaded adjective gives away a similar 'suspicion' about small town dwellers – that they are *subject to* this limited environment; that its physical dimensions have somehow inveigled their way into the way they think and that the mind contracts to fit the living space allowed it.

In city writing, the cityscape itself, its very physicality, invariably impresses itself upon the narrative – as was borne out by the previous collection in this series, *Decapolis: Tales from Ten Cities*. The narrative element that structured those city stories was 'the encounter', the chance crossing of two strangers' paths facilitated by the city itself; here, as we shall see, the characters we come across in small town stories are generally firmly enmeshed already in pre-existing relationships, associations and routines. The characters we

INTRODUCTION

meet here are usually already friends, colleagues, relatives, lovers, neighbours, not strangers, and the 'structures' they encounter and negotiate are rarely physical. Even in the stories where seemingly random encounters occur – the old man watching the female commuter every morning in Danielle Picard's story; the blind man meeting the broken-down train in 'Fog Island' – the reader gets the feeling that even these encounters have been ritualised or planned out. We doubt that the blind man's walk in the fog to rescue lost travellers is his first, and even Frode Grytten's Morrissey fan's trip to the bus station to find a girlfriend from 'outside' is strategic in its own way. Even chance is codified.

In a city story, the device of 'the encounter' speaks of the multiple narratives and infinite possibilities engendered by city spaces, a place of individuation and of freedom. The common narrative element that marks these small town stories, however, is the need for a protagonist to negotiate their place *within* the structures that a small town nurtures. And therein lies the crux of small town writing – the small town, its physicality usually negated by its very nature as something of a generic space, unchanging and stable, becomes less important as a physical entity and more so as a metaphorical one. Many of the small towns here go unnamed, and some even appear to be imagined. Where cityscapes seem unavoidably to impose their material shape onto a story, the materiality of the small town drops into the background, throwing its social practices into relief.

The internal politics of small town life are perhaps the defining features that have contributed most to its adoption as a pejorative term. According to received wisdom, the small town is a place ruled by expectation and by obligation. It is a place where a certain reaction is required to certain events, and where who you know determines what you can do, and everyone's business is fair game for everyone else. It is a place where not rocking the boat, keeping the peace and following protocol is valued, it seems, above all else. 'It's all a matter of

INTRODUCTION

cliques,' as Ingo Schulze's narrator has it here, 'whether old or new.' Rules are rules; it's the way we've always done things here.

And the small town stories collected here don't shatter these preconceptions; their manoeuvres are more subtle than that. The spaces depicted and brought to life here *do* function in this way – each is subject to its own rules and regulations into which its inhabitants are inculcated, ranging from the sinister to the comedic; in Jean Sprackland's story, the local pub encourages underage drinkers as 'a long-term investment.' The politics of the shop queue in Olga Tokarczuk's story – patience and 'witty repartee' in return for baking ingredients – seems well-embedded in town life. And yet what these stories do challenge is the assumption that their dwellers are simply *subject* to these rules, that they possess no autonomy or control, or insight into their imposition. They separate 'small town' as an entity from 'small town' as an adjective, and in doing so undercut the idea that the social order is as stable and all-pervasive as it seems.

The small towns of these stories are not isolated tableaux. They are indeed 'elsewhere', on the periphery in terms of location and national importance, and the crises that take place there tend to appear deeply personal. But intertwined with personal fate is the wider 'state of the nation': economic problems, social issues, and so on. Compared to city-stories, the action has decamped from the streets to the domestic arena, but is arguably all the more sharply focused as social comment for this. The episode surrounding a bottle of soup in Olga Tokarczuk's story speaks volumes, for example, about the economic privations of small town Poland. Small towns arguably most keenly feel the effects of economic (if not social) change, and are seemingly equipped with the least flexibility to adapt. The delicate edifices of small town life continually come under scrutiny in these stories, and their flaws become obvious: in Mehmet Zaman Saçlıoğlu's 'Fog Island', the café that is open 24 hours

INTRODUCTION

a day, a pillar of the community, is closed on the day it is most needed. In Olga Tokarczuk's story, the need to pin down the paternity of an illegitimate child is less a personally pressing matter than a logistically pressing one; the child cannot be baptised without a father's name, but no-one seems in the least outraged or surprised that a young girl can fall pregnant and suspect any number of men to be the father.

Because of the repeated 'failure' of these small towns' social institutions, a sense of melancholy infuses a number of these stories. Their inhabitants can sense the hypocrisy in adhering to 'rules' that obviously don't work, but at the same time, they're unwilling to completely let go of the idealistic vision of the small town – what in American fiction would be the lure of the white picket fence. Some of these stories hang oddly between this idealism and a more gritty reality; Frode Grytten's protagonist struggles between his 'inner picture' of his home town, 'a dirty and rusty and old Odda, but a beautiful Odda all the same', and the town it's becoming in reality, 'trying to be Not-Odda'. In Gyrðir Elíasson's 'The Water People', this tension shows itself in the odd disparity between the story's mythical tone and its quotidian subject matter. These towns are subject to the double vision of their inhabitants; it's a love-hate relationship.

The small town setting comes to function in these stories as a cipher for other types of structure and stricture, a shorthand for negotiating within boundaries imposed from elsewhere: as a location it throws up family problems, friendships, marriages, neighbourly disputes, community-wide crises. The small town, with its rigid codes of behaviour, become analogous to the situations and states of its characters, to adolescence, to old age, to redundancy, each arriving with their own sets of expected reactions. In coming to terms with and challenging the logic of the small town and its politics, the protagonists of these stories often crave spaces with none, or with alternative rules of their own: in Jean Sprackland's story, the narrator and her friends gravitate towards a man

INTRODUCTION

they don't like, but who has 'his own flat,' and is 'unencumbered by parents and siblings.' In Micheál Ó Conghaile's 'The Closeted Pensioner', a retired civil servant opts out in extremis, and creates his own idealised space in the downstairs toilet of his house. Ingo Schulze's househusband, pinioned by the routine of his work-replacement household chores and the fine specimen of functional masculinity next door, drifts so far from the reality of his situation into an alternate and skewed one that the reader is no longer sure what to believe.

It's in these small slices of a kind of freedom – these deviations from the script – that these stories' protagonists come to reveal themselves. They employ various strategies to resist or disassemble the structures imposed upon them, to varying degrees. At one end of the spectrum are the tiny, linguistic resistances – the distinct difference between what is said and what is meant. The wind could blow straight through a number of the conversations in these stories, but so much more is said than is spoken outright. Many of the narrative devices used are marked by ellipsis, suppression, obfuscation, double meaning; information is withheld, things are left unsaid, white lies are told. In Mirja Unge's story, it is only the repetitions of 'on the bus' that punctuate the narrator's train of thought that make clear that great swathes of the story she at first appears to tell her friend are actually for our ears only. This story is one in which we are privy to the narrator's innermost thoughts; just as often we are not. In Roman Simić's piece, for example, the ellipses are left to stand and speak for themselves. In Danielle Picard's story, a mother's joy in singing remains unknown to her daughter until after her death and complicates the daughter's sense of her mother, previously so firmly held. In places whose social economy depends on *knowing all*, holding back can be a powerful tool.

At the other end of the spectrum, the small town story seems in some way genetically predisposed to turn towards

INTRODUCTION

surrealism. The messiness and strangeness of real life, when put under pressure, bursts the banks of societal convention and leaks out in all sorts of ways. Elements of several stories here teeter on the edge of the real and the surreal: Ingo Schulze's protagonist's increasingly odd narrative lens, Micheál Ó Conghaile's pensioner's absolute conviction that moving into the downstairs toilet is a way to escape death, the distinctly blurred view of the world through replica Morrissey glasses in Frode Grytten's 'Sing Me to Sleep'. There are impulses, desires, private passions, even neuroses and psychoses that need to find expression – a space outside the 'small town' – and the surrealist bent of some of these stories allow that side some space. They show protagonists 'bleeding the radiator', as Ingo Schulze's narrator has it, letting off steam; these stories are at heart about *managing* those desires and passions, and transgressing the rules every once in a while in order to be able to stick to them the rest of the time.

So the mind of a small town protagonist doesn't contract to fit its environment; quite the opposite. It seeks out its own space despite the confines of the physical environment. It is agile and manipulative and idealistic all at once.

And the shape of the short story itself comes to mirror the shape of life in a small town. Its narratives are resistant, unfinished. Its 'resolutions' are rarely that; they overspill the boundaries of the stories, which 'end' at the beginning of conversations, with opaque hints, with deceptions. Those which appear to offer harmonious conclusions on the surface, when examined a little more closely, merely add another layer to the construction. These are stories which ramify far beyond the space they take up on the page, and do so in both temporal directions. They are designed to appear infinitely long, as if we as readers have walked in on a process that was begun a very long time ago, and will not be finished for a long time yet.

Pivoting on small defiances, small deviations and odd idiosyncrasies, these stories show that even where there is

INTRODUCTION

only the smallest room for manoeuvre, it's possible to keep a piece of oneself private; to construct a space which is one's own. The short story is a form which is so finely tuned, where every word makes its presence felt and is absolutely necessary, that's it's perfectly suited to giving these tiny manipulations the prominence and detail they require. It lends itself equally to getting inside the mindset of an isolated individual, but is at the same time a form comfortable to let silences stand, to leave things unspoken.

For better or for worse, it's the small details and gestures – a white lie, the turning of a blind eye, a small kindness or a secret kept – that allow a small town community to continue within their self-imposed systems for survival but at the same time to live as flawed human beings.

It's how we do things here, elsewhere.

Maria Crossan, Sept 07.

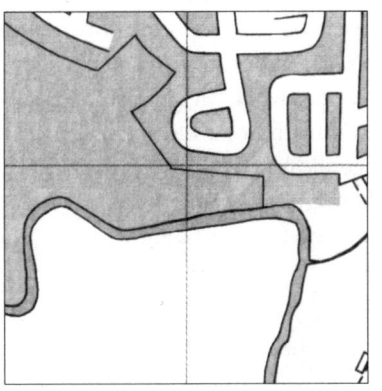

It was just, Yesterday

Mirja Unge

If I run at five to eight I'm just in time for the bus and sitting on the bus as usual is that Down's kid and he's the King of the Bus. He goes right to the last stop at the special school, so he sits there shouting all the time, he does it every morning when you get on and this morning too of course.

Welcome onto the bus, you with the black hair, he calls out, because he keeps tabs on people and his tongue sticking out a little way.

Where d'you get the air from, I say once I've reached the back of the bus where he is sitting with his legs splayed wide and his hair slicked down and I don't look in his direction because I've like seen him before. He laughs and slaps his bus pass on his thigh, I sit on one of the seats in front of him and check my hair in my little mirror, there it is jet black on my head. It's only one stop to where Thea gets on and she'd said fucking hell it looks really cool when I dyed it and black suited me she said and pulled her fingers through it Thea did.

The bus pulls in by the church and Thea and her brother get on and Thea's cropped her hair all over so her neck and throat you can't take your eyes off them.

Welcome onto the bus, shouts the King of the Bus and Thea's done her lips purple.

Thanks mate, she says and sits across the aisle from me.
Where d'you get the air from, says the King of the Bus.
I just breathed in simple as that, says Thea.

Thea and I roll fags on the bus, the tobacco crumbles and feels rough between your fingers and Thea's got earrings with skulls a row of them right along her earlobe and I laugh.

What're you laughing for, asks Thea.

Oh it was just, yesterday, I say.

Did you manage to get any, she says, and leans back against the window and puts her legs up on the seat with her trainers out in the aisle.

No feet on seats, shouts the King of the Bus and Thea snorts and so do I.

No it didn't work out, I say.

So did you get any or what, says Thea and I shrug, because I stood outside the off-licence for two bloody hours trying to get somebody to buy me some, the best bet are usually the young ones you can show off to and giggle with a bit so they soften up and start asking to swap phone numbers and I usually give them the maths teacher's number because I know that one off by heart now. It was just as I was standing there trying then one of those winos came up and asked what I wanted, and I gave him two hundred and my feet were so cold, it was freezing. And then some guys came over and started talking and I kept an eye on the door of the off-licence I'm sure I did, but he never came out and I didn't get it because he'd gone in but he didn't come and then the place shut and one of those guys he'd bought a fair bit of the wine, he said it, that I could have a bottle of his and I mean that was dead nice of him.

Some wino did a runner with the money, I say to Thea on the bus.

You're not serious, she said.

But I got a bottle of wine from another guy that was cool of him wasn't it, I say and Thea, she goes

fucking hell, he took the whole two hundred?

IT WAS JUST, YESTERDAY

The bus slams on the brakes for an elk or something, it's obviously deer trotting across the road into the forest and Thea's rolling fags, Thea's painted her nails green and there's a scent floating about in everything that's hers, her clothes and room and hair, lovely and soft it's there.

Fucking hell he took the whole two hundred, says Thea.

Yeah but I did get that wine anyhow, I say.

Was it red then or what, says Thea.

Don't know.

Didn't you look, she says and I stare out of the window and say I left it at his place.

You what.

I left it at his place, I say and her eyes are fixed on me, they're green with streaks of brown in the middle she's got black mascara and she has this allergy so her nose is blocked nearly all the time.

The bus pulls in at the market garden and all the people standing there crowd on pushing and shoving.

Welcome onto the bus, shouts the King of the Bus and I yell at him to

shut up.

Where d'you get the air from, he says.

She just got it, get it, says Thea and the bus moves off and pulls out into the road again. Thea's eyes on me.

You went home with him, she says and I nod and she gathers up her tobacco and bag and everything and shifts across and sits down next to me, I squeeze up to make room and I'm in her scent drifting and perfumey around her. I can feel my feet are all cold and numb, my legs are sort of heavy just like they were when I went with him, because he said I should come up to his for a bit, he was absolutely bloody sure he knew who that wino was who'd pissed off with the money, and if I just came up for a while he'd ring round and check it out, because I wanted my money back didn't I and he was sure as hell he knew who'd ripped me off. He rabbited on about that wino who was obviously a total nutter and I walked beside him and I didn't need to, I could get the bus home and ring Thea and I could've had her voice against my ear almost right inside me, but I went with him freezing and listening to his spiel and the bottles chinking together in the bag he was carrying. He tapped in the door code and yanked open the main door and I went up the stairs after him and I could have turned round but I didn't turn round I waited behind him while he unlocked the door.

And, says Thea nudging me and I wiggle my feet because there's no feeling in them.

Well see, I sneer, he had this shitty bedsit with an eighties fan on the ceiling right and a fitted carpet, I say. And it was bloody cold out by then but it was warm up there and he poured me a whisky and I drank it and it warmed me up inside and all over. I giggled and got warm, but my feet were cold, really freezing. He was going to ring the wino he said, first he put some music on, Iron Maiden it was and that whisky went to my head because I'd hardly had anything since school dinner and I didn't know I didn't realise until he was sitting there with me on the sofa and he had on some fragrance for men and he worked for a computer firm somewhere and he stroked my hair, it was nice his hand on my hair.

What did you do at his place then, says Thea and licks the edge of her cigarette paper.

Drank whisky, I say. Flipping hell, whisky works quick, I laugh, and Thea laughs too, her breasts bob up and down under her jumper because she doesn't think you should shut things up in bras or cages, she's a vegetarian and sometimes yells at old women wearing fur coats in the street. And the night before yesterday, when we were sitting up in Thea's room in the roof that's got a sloping ceiling so you can't sit upright on the bed, when we were lying there she laughed and I said,

your breasts bob up and down when you laugh.

Don't tell me you're lying there looking at my breasts, she says.

Why not, they're bobbing around having a good time right in front of my eyes, how can I not, I said.

What d'you mean? said Thea, they're not that big.

Nah course not, I said.

You saying they're small then, she asked, propping herself up on her elbow.

No definitely not.

But they look small that's what you think isn't it, she said and suddenly pulled up her top so her breasts were taken totally unawares and sat there exposed with their paleness, are they small, do you think, she said and squeezed and weighed one of them in her hand.

I leant across and put my hand over, placed my hand carefully so my palm was pressed against her and her breast felt sort of hot.

They're too small, aren't they, said Thea and I took my hand away and managed to get some saliva to trickle down and wet my throat.

They're just the way they should be, I said. I'm absolutely sure in fact that they're exactly the way they should be, right. She pulled down her top and sat on the edge of the bed.

Though there's always the chance they'll grow a bit more, she said.

And I sit there on the bus looking at her laughter, looking at her eyes.

The bus goes past the pig farm and the stink of the pigs seeps in through the windows and round the edges and fills every breath you take and the King of the Bus giggles at the back and shouts out.

Who's farting on the bus.

Shut your mouth, I yell and Thea gets her little bottle of perfume out of her bag and sprays it into the air.

Was he good-looking, that boy, says Thea and I rack my brains to remember anything about how he looked because everybody has to look some way or another, all I had to do was remember, but I couldn't, all I could think of was the way he smiled when we were standing in the kitchen and I asked if he was going to ring that wino who legged it with the cash, I mean the way he smiled just then and said I was pretty, and sometimes Thea says that, sometimes she comes up and gives me a hug and sometimes she laughs and wants us to kiss, and when I was standing in his kitchen he suddenly leant forward and kissed me on the mouth and I didn't have time to see it coming or realise before he'd done it and then it was already over and I staggered a bit and he held on to me because he had quite strong arms and a white T-shirt with a Lacoste crocodile.

So come on, what did he look like, says Thea on the bus and I shrug.

Quite good-looking I s'pose.

I can't believe you left the bottle of wine, she says.

What, I say.

The wine, how could you leave it at his place.

Oh, I must have been too pissed, I say and laugh and she laughs too and the bus rattles and I forgot the bottle of wine I didn't think about it, I walked out, walked slowly because it was hurting somewhere it was empty and some huge damn lonely thing was just swelling and swelling and I didn't realise I didn't know because I hadn't said anything, I hadn't pushed away his body I'd just lain there on the sofa and it had felt like my belly and crotch were bursting when he came in and Iron Maiden were screaming and my head was thumping against the arm of the sofa thump thump against the arm and I didn't say anything I didn't do anything but I was there with my head against the arm and Iron Maiden and the whisky in my head thump thump.

My feet did what they were told and walked the way they usually do across the tarmac towards the bus stop, but I forgot the bottle of wine I forgot it, I knew I'd forgotten something, I just couldn't remember what.

He took me, I'm not a virgin any more, I say.

IT WAS JUST, YESTERDAY

Never. You got there before me then, hisses Thea. I press the stop button and the bus swings into the turning place outside the school.

Welcome back onto the bus tomorrow, shouts the King of the Bus and I turn and yell

where d'you get the air from?

C'mon then, what was it like, says Thea shaking my arm, and I shrug and look out of the window.

Nice I guess.

Translated from the Swedish by Sarah Death

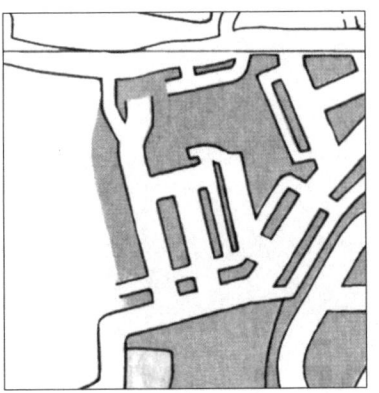

My Career in Goodness

Jean Sprackland

Sunday morning, seven forty-five, and I was frying eggs – twenty-eight of them – and slapping each one between two slices of white bread and marge. A familiar routine, but not what I felt like doing after three hours' sleep under a leather jacket in someone's basement. The whites of the eggs were wobbling like fat, but the heat of the pan firmed and whitened them and then I could just about stand it.

When I handed round the tea, they gazed at me with their beautiful smiles. Lillian, Miss Bond, the Rector... they looked up at me as if I was an angel. I felt a stab of shame: they seemed so innocent, so unworldly, they didn't know my eyes were gritty and my stomach was frothing violently and I could feel cystitis coming on again.

'Put me a bit more sugar in mine, will you duck?'

'As much as you like, Jessie. She's at church.'

'Church! That one! She wouldn't know God from a bar of soap.'

At this mention of the Almighty, the Rector began to tremble violently and spilled his tea on his trousers. Fortunately the tea here was always lukewarm.

It was September, my third month working in this place. I'd walked out of school in the middle of my History O Level, after staring blankly at the paper for some time, unable to recall anything whatsoever about the Reunification of Italy. I'd had more than enough of school in any case. I decided it was time for me to start living instead. I closed the question booklet, put down my pencil and walked out.

She was Mrs Wyman, a Dutch woman of indeterminate age. She ruled this place like a concentration camp, and I only began to see why when she cornered me in the sluice one afternoon and described her wartime experiences. I stood there, uncertain whether to go on folding towels or pay full attention. You wouldn't generally let Mrs Wyman see you idle, but on this occasion she didn't seem to notice; in fact she was hardly aware of my presence, she was so intent on her story. If I hadn't happened to be there, I think she would have told the empty room, the buckets and bedpans. She had been a young woman, seventeen years old, in Amsterdam during the Nazi occupation. You couldn't get bicycle tyres so they had to ride around on the steel rims. When the food ran out, they ate tulip bulbs. She said if you'd ever eaten boiled tulip bulbs you would never forget the taste.

I understood her a little better afterwards. Her harshness, her puritanism were no easier to live with, but at least I knew they weren't random things; she'd been damaged for life by those traumatic youthful experiences. In particular, they had left her fanatically intolerant of waste of any kind —waste of time, waste of space, but especially waste of food. Every uneaten scrap must be saved, and the fridge was always full of chipped little bowls, each containing a teaspoonful of peas or mashed potato, until at the end of the week she came along and scraped them all into the bits bowl. Everything in that bowl went back into the supper on Friday night.

I may have been an angel by day, but by night I was learning to be bad. I hadn't yet worked out what it meant to start living; I had no vision for my future. But I knew I'd never get anywhere in this world without knowing how to be bad. The local options were limited, but at least this town was famous for its pubs. It used to be said that there were more pubs here per head of the population than anywhere else in England... but isn't that what they all say, these proud, hard-drinking towns, all jacked up and no place to go? Anyhow there was plenty of choice, and the ones we liked were the real dives: the Swan, the Railway, the Dog. You'd walk in, and there'd be a very particular smell – a mixture of cigarette smoke, slops and cheap air-freshener – and you'd take a long, deep breath. It was the smell of home.

I was balancing all that out by working here. I'd get the first bus home, change into my scratchy navy-blue overall without even washing, take my bike out of the shed and cycle to work. I worked the bad clean out of me, scrubbing sheets till my hands bled, then I went home and put on skinny jeans still damp off the radiator, and a black vest top, and spike heels. I lit the first cigarette of the evening, and walked out into air that smelled of privet and ruined pork chop dinners.

And this is how the summer was sliding by: long days at work, long evenings in the pub, long nights back at someone's flat. Mad drinking games, like the time one of the lads challenged Rob Trickett to hold a full pint by gripping the edge of the glass between his teeth, and then we took turns to pick the splinters out of his tongue, and he couldn't feel a thing. Or our favourite, the one where we stood in a solemn circle, passing a mouthful of Marston's Pedigree one to the next, until it grew so warm, so flat and so diluted with saliva that someone would find it impossible to hold it for the regulation count of five and would spit it out into a glass (if there was one handy). Of course, this weird game, surely revolting to everyone outside the circle, was nothing more than a pretext to get very intimate: boys with girls, boys with boys, girls with girls. Look at the way you had to hold your partner's head, gentle but close, to keep it still and your mouths docked as you dribbled the liquid in. We were so in love with each other, and with ourselves.

'Excuse me, young lady...' The Rector forgot my name every day and was too proud to ask it. Even with his stoop, he was a tall man. He still had a sort of floppy white fringe, which gave him a boyish look completely at odds with his arthritis and his dementia. 'I wonder whether you're familiar with Aristotle on the subject of matter and form? The cup of tea, for instance.' He nodded towards Miss Bond, who had poured her tea into the saucer, a practice which was strictly forbidden here. 'See how the matter – that is, the tea itself – has been separated, or isolated, from the form – the "cup of tea". Is this not a most elegant demonstration of Aristotle's concept of *ousia*, or substance?'

'You're right, Rector. It's potentiality and actuality, isn't it?'

If anyone had been listening, they might have been impressed. What they wouldn't have known is that the Rector and I had almost exactly the same exchange yesterday, when I took breakfast up to his room. While he found his copy of *Metaphysics*, and fumbled the pages looking for the reference, I hooked two pairs of filthy underpants with my foot from under the bed and stuffed them in the pocket of my overall. We all had a right to our secrets.

I was learning a lot from the Rector. I was aware of the irony of learning philosophy from a man who was gaga more than half the time. His short-term memory was so poor, he often demanded breakfast even as I cleared it away. If I showed him his empty porridge bowl, he would be hurt, outraged, accuse me of tricking him, of trying to starve him. I learnt it was easier to go along with him, to say 'You're right, I'm ever so sorry – I'll get it right away.' Two minutes later he'd have forgotten. These small deceptions were a way of life, essential in getting us all through each hour of each day. At first I was resistant to them. I had principles, and one of them was that these people should retain their dignity, that we owed them the truth. But there was no dignity in the rage and terror my fanatical honesty brought bubbling to the surface. I learnt to lie, smoothly and convincingly. I learnt to say what they wanted to hear.

The Rector was, in many ways, an odd choice of mentor. He was one of our more difficult residents: often confused, truculent, even aggressive. He over-estimated his own physical strength; he would announce his intention to walk into town and fetch the police, but would make it only to the front gate and have to be coaxed back indoors, ashen and trembling and speaking in a defeated voice about 'this wicked place.' But at times in between he was lucid and ferociously clever, and would lecture me about the great thinkers. At first I found this baffling, then intimidating. But one day, as I was making his bed, he began to talk about theory of knowledge, or epistemology, and questioning me about how I knew that the sheets were white or that the sun would rise in the morning. Gradually these conversations became important, like shiny threads in the dark fabric of my days here. He had identified something in me, some readiness to listen. I was struggling to understand anything at all about Wittgenstein and language games, but I really felt I was getting to grips with rationalism and empiricism. Even the vocabulary of philosophy was exotic somehow – it spoke of another, more varied world, a world of open horizons, of questions so wide and so deep I had never even imagined they could be asked. It spoke of the possibility of *escape*.

The landlords of our down-at-heel pubs were surprisingly tolerant; I suppose we were already good business, and encouraging us in our under-age drinking represented a long-term investment. Eventually, though, a bell would ring behind the bar and it would be Time. Then there was a bit of a scramble to find somewhere to go; this town, for all its bravado, lacked formal facilities for after-hours drinking.

Tonight, as on many nights, we settled on Colin Hick's place. Colin was in his twenties – well past it – but we maintained a strategic relationship with him because he had his own flat. It was an appalling place, but it was within staggering distance of the Swan, and importantly he was unencumbered by parents and siblings. We could do anything we liked there without fear of detection.

He looked especially unkempt when he opened the door to us tonight. His beard (yuk) had a greasy look, and his eyes were bloodshot. He said he had a few friends round and yes of course we could hang out with them. Julie was whispering something in my ear, reminding me to watch him – her boyfriend had called round one afternoon to pick up a record he'd left the night before and found Colin in bed with two girls from the year below us at school (yuk double yuk). Anyway you could tell he was genuinely pleased to see us, all twelve of us, tottering and giggling on his doorstep. He was a bit of a misfit, and these regular invasions by drunken teenagers brought colour to his life.

We helpfully despatched all the alcohol on the premises, including his toxic homebrew. Then suddenly it was the early hours of the morning, and I was out in the yard with an anonymous stranger, who was insisting on lifting me by the waist and perching me on a parked Kawasaki, the better to get his hands on my erogenous zones.

'No no can't rideamotobikle,' I protested, and slid gracelessly off into a heap on the ground. The chivalrous one, apparently deciding I was too far gone to be any fun, wandered off, and I lay for a while on the concrete and gazed at the sky. There was a rough moon wandering in and out of thin, silvery clouds. After a time the cold of the ground had seeped up through me, and I gathered myself somehow and staggered back into the flat, through the kitchen and into a small back room. It was warm and quiet in here, and so smoky that it took me a moment to discern the half-dozen or so figures sitting on the floor, leaning against the walls. A friendly-looking boy patted a space on the floor next to him and I sat down. There was a very odd scent in here – dangerous and comforting at the same time. When a big, loosely rolled cigarette was passed to me, it seemed polite to take an enormous drag. A few seconds later I came round with my head in the nice boy's lap and smouldering ash on my jeans.

'I'm drunk,' I blurted apologetically.

'Hello Drunk, I'm Robert.'

'Robert. What are you?'

'I'm going to be a psychiatrist. What about you?'

I hesitated. I couldn't possibly tell him about my day job.

'I'm studying philosophy,' I said, and I thought it sounded all right.

'Ah. Jean-Paul Sartre?'

'Pardon?'

His eyes were of the most extraordinary blue, but I had begun to feel at a disadvantage. It took a great effort to lift my head from his lap and sit upright.

'Kiss me, Robert.'

He did, and his tongue was in my mouth straight away, not a bit like the careful, businesslike kisses of the lads at school. This was something new. When he broke off to tell me I had great-tasting teeth, it absolutely sealed my fate, since I'd always been rather shy about the unevenness of my teeth and tried to hide them whenever I could – our family albums were full of photographs of me with my mouth clamped shut.

He was two years older than me. He was waiting for his A Level results and he had a summer job at the heel bar in the indoor market. He asked for my number, and I gave him the work one; it would have been unthinkable to have him call me at home. Every time the phone rang I raced to get there first and then let it ring three times at least before seizing the receiver and saying hello in my most nonchalant voice, remembering to lower the pitch a tone or two. But it was never him.

The house where I worked was a Victorian mansion on a hill on the edge of town. It was the kind of house some of the residents, in their earlier lives, with the war over at last and families and mortgages to look after, might have dreamed of inhabiting. There was a huge lawn with flowerbeds, and a gravel drive lined with horse-chestnut trees, and three whitewashed steps up to a handsome front door flanked by stone pillars. This door was never used, except when the undertaker came. Then Mrs Wyman would reach up to a high shelf over the mirror in the dining room, and fetch down a big key, and the heavy oak door would creak open, and light and air flood into the hall.

Round the back was a yard with washing lines strung across it, and a lean-to where I parked my bike, alongside several rusty lawnmowers and an old mangle. I'd nip in through the servants' entrance, hoping Mrs Wyman wouldn't intercept me and complain about some misdemeanour on my previous shift. There was always something. Didn't I realise I'd left a wet tea-towel on the kitchen table? How many times did she have to tell me to check down the back of Jessie's armchair for pills?

The Rector hadn't been well, and I called in to check on him. He had the best bedroom in the house; in spite of her general misanthropy Mrs Wyman retained a steely respect for him, because he was a man of the cloth and highly educated. It faced west, with a view over open fields to the Derbyshire hills beyond. He had a row of books on the shelf, and had even been allowed to bring his own writing desk and install it in front of the window.

'Ah, come in and take a seat,' he said in a genial tone of voice. 'I'm just about to make some notes.'

There was a red diary on the desk, with *1953* in gold block lettering on the cover. He turned the pages with a shaking hand, and I saw the days with their neat handwritten appointments, some in pencil, others in proper ink. It was the hand of a much younger man that had made them. As he turned a page, a photograph fell out.

'Is that you, Rector?'

'Mmm? I suppose it must be. Oh, yes.' It was tiny, smaller than a passport photo. He held it very close to his eyes. 'I've lost my spectacles.'

'Can I look?'

The black and white image sent a stab of shock through me. A smiling young man in a clerical collar, holding a puppy in his arms. An older woman in a flowery dress, laughing up at him. Everything about it was startling: the smile, the tenderness of his expression, the domesticity of it. Somehow it had never occurred to me that there had been people and things in his life: family, pets, a garden with an apple tree.

'Who is she?'

'He, not she. We called him Treacle.'

'I meant the lady, not the dog!'

'Oh, that's my mother. This was taken on her birthday, look – April 19th. That's why I keep it in here.'

'She looks lovely. So happy. And you, with a church of your own and everything.'

He gave a non-committal grunt.

'I was wondering,' I said carefully. 'Do you still read the Bible and all that? Is it still something you... He was by nature such a sceptic, it was difficult to imagine him believing in God, never mind delivering a sermon or leading a congregation in prayer.

He took the photograph from me and put it back between the pages. He was muttering something about Nietzsche and *Death of God Theology*.

'I've never heard of that. Death of God – I mean, how can you be a vicar and talk about the death of God?'

He gave me an icy look.

'Hadn't you better be getting back to work? I pay you to type up my letters, not to stand about gossiping.'

After two weeks I couldn't stand any more of the tension. Perhaps he'd accidentally washed my number off his hand before he had the chance to write it down? On my day off I went to the indoor market. I loved everything about this place, especially the old-fashioned toy stall which sold elaborate string puppets I used to yearn for as a child; seeing them now in the window I felt again that ache of desire, remarkably similar to the feeling I had for Robert. I played for time, browsing the arcane goods on offer at the haberdashery stall, the cheese stall, the handbag and purse stall. And there it was, Keys Cut and Heel Bar, on the corner of my vision as I lurked behind a display of flannelette sheets. A man in blue dungarees was cutting a key: the sparking of metal on the wheel, and a hot smell that mingled excitingly with the smells of ham and fish and leather from the surrounding stalls. But I didn't have a plan of action, and paradoxically I was terrified Robert might spot me.

Next door to the heel bar there was a greasy spoon café where you could sit on a high stool and drink milky coffee. I perched there and took out my copy of *Existentialism and Humanism*. I was there for a very long time, making the horrible coffee last, so determined not to look up even for a moment that the lines on the page were as stolid as bricks in a wall and the sound of keys on the wheel was like an agonised shriek of torture. When eventually I sneaked a look, there was still no Robert, just the man in dungarees. He was switching off the machines and fetching a broom. I shoved the book in my bag and scurried over.

'Excuse me, I'm looking for Robert.'

'Sorry duck, we're shut.'

'I don't want anything. It's about Robert.'

'Who?' He didn't bother to look up from his sweeping.

'He works here. Is he ill?'

'Oh, the lad. Robert, isn't it?'

'Yes, that's what I said.'

'Ah. He's gone, duck.'

I was close to screaming point. 'What do you mean *gone*?'

'University. Going to be a brain surgeon, I reckon. He's

not going to mend shoes all his life, is he? Meant for higher things, that one.' He glanced up at me and gave a short, nasty laugh. 'Three years spongeing off the taxpayer first though eh?'

'I don't like the look of him,' said Mrs Wyman, nodding towards the Rector. He had a cough, and he'd been awkward and out of sorts all week. This afternoon he'd brought a toilet roll into the dining room, and was shredding it systematically and stuffing the pieces into his teacup. We knew him well enough to predict that this sort of compulsive behaviour often preceded one of his rages. 'Perhaps I should prepare the shot, just in case.'

'Mmm,' I said dubiously. More than anything, I hated that routine: holding him down, sitting on his chest if necessary, while Mrs Wyman unfastened his hopeless trousers and injected largactyl into his thigh. The flesh there was veined like cheese. After a few seconds he'd stop struggling and lie still and docile at last. It was just like watching something die.

'Would you like me to try and calm him down first?' I was careful to sound capable rather than pleading. She would not tolerate any sign of weakness, but she knew that I was good with this troublesome man, that there was a special bond between us. She didn't like it, but it was useful.

I went and sat beside him. He was concentrating very hard, and he didn't look up. The floppy fringe was damp with sweat. I watched him tear off a sheet of paper, fold it in half lengthways, then in half widthways, then in half again lengthways, then unfold it and tear along the creases. It's difficult to tear toilet paper neatly, even without arthritic fingers, and he was making a little snort of irritation with each breath. I would have liked to put my hand on his, to make him stop, but I knew better than to touch him.

'I've been reading that book you lent me,' I said tentatively.

More tearing. More snorting.

'You know, *The Concept of Mind*. Rye, is it?'

'Ryle,' he barked, without glancing up from his task.

'Ryle, that's right. I – er – I like what he says about Cartesian Dualism. The ghost in the machine. I'll have to read it again before I really get it, of course. But I think he's on to something...'

He stopped abruptly and turned to me with a look of absolute disdain.

'Gilbert Ryle was the greatest of the logical behaviourists,' he said fiercely. 'His importance in twentieth century thought is second only to Wittgenstein, and that book is a masterwork.'

'Really? I had no idea.'

'*And* he was a great Plato scholar, scandalously underrated.' He threw down the remains of the toilet roll and began to heave himself to his feet. He wanted so much to stalk out, to make the arrogant gesture. I helped him push the chair back and then busied myself tidying up so that I wouldn't have to witness his slow, unsteady journey to the door.

It was a victory. Mrs Wyman rewarded me by saying that since it was a quiet afternoon I could clean the front porch. It meant a cool, peaceful half-hour, a chance to recover from the hangover which had been creeping and spreading all day, and to think about Robert. I missed him, even though I'd never got to know him. In fact, not knowing him made it easier to miss him – it was pure and absolute feeling, undiluted by any actual memories. There were none of the usual complications or uncertainties, no awkward recollections to cringe over, no moments of boredom or disagreement or jealousy. In some ways it really had been the perfect relationship. There he was in my mind's eye: clever, funny, a good kisser. He had brilliant blue eyes. Best of all, he had left this town for the bigger world I knew was out there – a world of ethics and meta-ethics, ontology and personal identity. He had walked out and started living.

I took down a tall earthenware vase to dust it, and found there was something inside, something like crumpled black crepe paper. I went to the mirror in the dining room, reached up to the shelf and felt for the front door key. I carried the vase out into the sunshine and peered in. It was a small dead bat; the word *pipistrelle* came to mind. It must have flown or fallen in, and been unable to climb out because of the narrow neck and slippery sides of the vase. I stood for a long time looking at the broken shape of it, like a tiny package of elbows and rags shrouded in cobweb, and I was reminded somehow of Miss Haversham and the wedding dress. Then I tipped it out onto the flower-bed and scuffed a bit of soil over it with my foot.

When I came to work here, I could feel things, really feel them. Every day I was becoming harder, more like her. It frightened me.

Dinnertime. Once we'd got the relatively hale and hearty sitting at the table, I'd carry trays to the bed-ridden and the reclusive in their rooms. The Rector was not bed-ridden, but he certainly did suffer from reclusive moods, and his cough had been bad the past few days. As I climbed the stairs with his tray, I steeled myself for another dose of Kantian ethics. I really didn't feel in the mood. None of this stuff meant what it used to, now Robert had gone. I remembered something he said the night we met: *I'm getting out while I have the chance.* It was as if they were setting up roadblocks, and he'd be the last one to make it.

I didn't have a spare hand, so I just called *Knock knock* in the chirpiest voice I could summon, and walked in. He was sitting at his desk, with his back to me and one hand on an open book in front of him. He might well be reading, or thinking, or enjoying the view. But something about the slope of his shoulder told me straight away.

I stood in the doorway for a long time holding the tray. I tried to have thoughts about personal responsibility, or about the nature of consciousness, but they wouldn't form properly. Touching his shoulder, or moving round to look at his face, these simple actions were out of the question. Sunlight and shadow moved lazily on the walls, the shabby bedspread, the page, his liver-spotted hand. I could hear Maurice, the odd-job man, clattering about by the bins outside.

'Dinnertime!' I said brightly. My voice was flat and artificial, the way it was when I spoke to myself in the linen press, counting out draw sheets.

I took one small step into the room and put the tray on the bed. As I did so, I caught sight of my face in the wardrobe mirror: a thin, pale girl with crooked front teeth.

Mrs Wyman was at the sink, washing out empty margarine tubs.

'Well?'

'The Rector.'

'What does he want?'

She pulled out the plug and drew her red hands from the soapy water. They were like furious, gnarled little creatures.

I thought back to another day, one of our conversations, when he'd quoted some philosopher or other – Bertrand or Bernard Something – *Immortality is inevitably boring*. I recalled how he looked as he said it: how something about it seemed to strike him as humorous and a rare smile lit his face for a second or two.

I turned and walked out of the house, took my bike from the lean-to. Maurice was smoking by the bins, and he gave me a mock salute as I rode through the gates, but I didn't return the greeting.

I pedalled madly down the drive and onto the dual carriageway, in my nylon overall full of sparks.

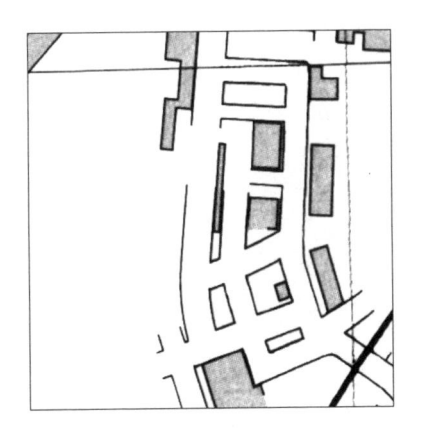

Sing Me to Sleep

FRODE GRYTTEN

I'm 40 now, the same age as Morrissey. Soon autumn will be here and my mother has come home to the flat in the Beehive to die. Most of the time she just lies in bed, cold and thin, tiny and transparent, waiting for death while she slips in and out of sleep.

I pull the duvet over her and get some water whenever she wants something to drink. I hold her hand and brush her hair when she's awake. I try to get her to take the pills she was given at the hospital, but she refuses.

'I've taken enough medicine,' she says. 'I don't want to take any more.'

I don't nag her, just tell myself that it doesn't really matter. It will soon be over anyway. Soon she will be gone.

I've moved the wing chair from the sitting room into her bedroom. I curl up in it with a blanket over me, when my mother is asleep. The days pass, bringing with them the last remnants of summer, flaring up for a final fling, before autumn turns everything into ash and decay.

I like the late August evenings when the dark creeps back and the moon rolls up onto the ridge of the mountain. I don't know, the light summer nights somehow don't feel right. Like they've been washed on the wrong programme.

I long for autumn, for the darkness and rain on the

windowpanes when all the lights outside look like streaks of finger paint that someone has smudged on the window.

I see how the light in the room slowly changes, how all the objects make different shadows according to the time of day. I see the nights closing in, and insects fluttering helplessly against the lit lamps.

One night, I catch a moth in my hands, hold him and feel him flapping around against my palms, desperately from side to side. Then I let him go.

At night, I play old Smith songs on my Walkman: 'Back to the Old House' and 'Stretch Out and Wait' and 'Asleep'. I know that in the future, when I play these songs, I will think of my mother and the last days of her life. *Sing me to sleep, sing me to sleep.*

I see how small she has become. She is tiny, like a little girl, like she's gone the full cycle, from girl to woman and now back to girl again.

But she's still beautiful and I like watching her when she's asleep. The fine lines on her face. Her thin hands resting on top of the duvet, hands with blood vessels arranged in strange patterns beneath the paper-thin skin.

Death is slowly spreading through her body. Soon it will be done. Soon it will be over. Soon my mother will be gone. For several days and nights she has inhabited a place somewhere between this world and another, where she will be beyond hope.

What has her life been like?

I remember something Morrissey once said about being happy. He said that it is impossible for a person to be truly happy. All your life you strive to be happy, but you can never achieve it, because you put aside all that is important, you put off all the things that are important while you wait for that day in your life that will never come.

I want to ask my mother about it, but I can't bring myself to. The words are too big, they'd get stuck in my throat and I'd die before her. I haven't even told her I love her, I haven't even dared to say something so small.

And yet I love her with all my heart. I really do love her, love her as much as a guy like me can love another person.

She is the best woman I know. I have never heard her say a bad word about anyone. Even after she divorced my father, she never had a harsh word to say about him. And I could think of a thousand bad things to say about my father.

I have so many mean words. My mother has none.

My mother has always sacrificed herself for others. She has put her own life to one side and has never even dreamt of the day that would never come. My whole life I've been a disappointment to her, but she has never criticised me. She has supported me in everything I've done.

For a while, I had a job with the Post Office and when I repeatedly refused to wear the uniform, they wanted to sack me. I asked them if they had any complaints about my work. Had someone complained, was there anyone who hadn't got their post or anything like that?

No, that wasn't the problem, it was simply that I had to wear the uniform when I was delivering the post, I couldn't wear a dark suit and T-shirt.

'This isn't just a T-shirt,' I said. 'It's my *Smiths* T-shirt.' Makes no difference, they told me, I couldn't wear a T-shirt when I was delivering the post, I had to wear the uniform. And I certainly could not go around with a bunch of daffodils in my back pocket. That was definitely highly irregular. It was just not on, to go around with a bunch of daffodils in your back pocket. I had to wear the uniform.

'But this is my uniform,' I said. 'Has anyone not got their post because I wear a Smiths T-shirt or have daffodils in my back pocket?' I told them that I thought they were scared of people with daffodils in their back pocket.

They fired me on the spot. So my mother went straight to the boss and got him to take me on again. Two weeks later I quit. My mother said nothing. There was nothing to discuss. I just had to leave.

I mean, I can't have a normal job; I can't get up at seven every morning to talk rubbish to people I hate. I can't have a job where I have to be with all those awful people and what's more, ask them what they're going to do at the weekend. *In my life, why do I smile, at people who I'd much rather kick in the eye?*

It's midnight. There's a full moon outside. My mother is asleep. I have just been to get her a glass of water. She has drunk it and gone back to sleep. I think that if my mother dies today she will die on the same day as Princess Diana, exactly one year after Diana crashed in Paris. That would be quite something.

My mother loved Princess Diana. I tease her about it and say that Princess Diana was just an incredibly boring woman with too much money. She did, of course, travel to the Third World every now and then and stroke poor children on the cheek and have her picture taken with them. But she was always dressed in Chanel, wasn't she?

I read out something Morrissey once said about Diana for my mother: that the princess spent £25,000 on make-up every year, and would a saint do that? For example, did Mother Teresa spend £25,000 a year on make-up? If Mother Teresa did spend £25,000 a year on make-up, she should get her money back immediately.

I play *Strangeways Here We Come* quietly on my Walkman. I don't know which Smiths' record I like best. It all depends. *The Queen Is Dead* is obviously the best; *The Queen Is Dead* is the best of absolutely all their records, but not always. Tonight *Strangeways* is just as good. Tonight I only want to play *Strangeways*.

My mother has always hated The Smiths. She's never said so straight out, but I know she hates them. And yet I have always been allowed to play my records as loud as I want. She's never asked me to turn down the volume or anything like that.

I once told her: 'Music is my only friend, music is the

only friend I've ever had.' She shook her head at that and gave me a hug.

She has never understood how you can become immersed in music and forget everything else. I remember the first time I heard The Smiths – I don't know, I think it's a feeling you search for over and over again for the rest of your life. But you can only be a virgin once, can't you?

Music is like breathing. I can be as down and depressed as is possible, but when I play certain records, it's as if I'm being slowly raised up from the floor and lifted to the ceiling. I read somewhere that Morrissey feels the same.

Music is the perfect opiate, Morrissey says. Music is better than drugs.

The clock radio flashes 00:45. My mother moans in her sleep; she is dreaming, I can tell by the way her eyes are moving under her eyelids. I wonder what she's dreaming about. What do you dream about when you know you're going to die? Everything that has happened? Everything that's going to happen? All the things that have never happened?

She wakes up and looks at me. I turn off the music and smile at her.

'You're a good boy,' she says. 'You've always been a good boy.'

I ask if she would like something more to drink. She shakes her head.

'It would be best for you if I were to die now,' she says.

I ask her not to say things like that, she's ill, talking rubbish.

'When I'm gone, you'll finally be free,' my mother says. 'Then you can go out and meet girls.'

'Don't say that, Mother!' I exclaim.

'I just want you to meet a nice girl, to meet someone you can marry and be happy with.'

She has never really grasped that. That there is no such thing as a happy marriage. Show me a happy couple and I'll send them a telegram with congratulations. Show me a harmonious family and I'll join the Foreign Legion.

My mother, of all people, should know that; she who split up with my father, who fought half her life with my father and then had to break all contact just to survive. Happiness cannot thrive in such restricted conditions.

'It would do you good to meet a girl,' my mother says.

'Go back to sleep,' I say.

She lies down.

I once read about Morrissey and his girlfriend in a magazine. While they were still together, the girl told their friends about everything that went on between her and Morrissey, everything, down to the most embarrassing details.

It was like hanging out your dirty laundry, Morrissey said and thought: Fine, I've had enough of this, I've had enough, this is not how I want to live. And apparently he's never been with anyone since. He's lived on his own. As the years passed, he realised: 'Well, I'm a celibate.'

I live like Morrissey. I'm a vegetarian and I'm celibate. I haven't had a girlfriend for twenty years. It's the only solution. *I will live my life as I will undoubtedly die – alone.* The world is so full of sex and so lacking in feeling. Most people keep their brains between their legs.

I hate it when people trivialise sex. I can't bring myself to talk about sex in a vulgar way. *Pussy talk,* that's what those gross men at the post office called it. Pussy talk. They made me sick. They were just a bunch of slavering morons. None of them had ever even heard of The Smiths.

My mother says she would like to know that there was someone there to look after me, to care for me.

'Imagine if you found yourself a nice girl,' she says.

God, we've talked about this a thousand times. She really wants a grandchild. That's the point. She doesn't want everything to die out with me. She wants things to continue, life should go on.

I wish with all my heart that I could be everything she wants me to be. I wish that I could, for once, not disappoint her. I would say anything to her, do anything for her, whatever, anything in the world, so she could die happy.

'I have got a girlfriend,' I say, and can't quite believe that I'm actually saying what I'm saying.

'I've got a girlfriend,' I say it again.

'You do?' my mother asks and pulls herself half up in the bed.

I nod.

'I haven't told you before now,' I continue. 'She's a bit shy.'

'But that's wonderful!' my mother says. 'How lovely. What's her name?'

'Marita,' I lie.

'Marita,' my mother repeats. 'How lovely! Does she live along the fjord?'

I say that her parents come from along the fjord, but that they don't live there any more. She lives here in Odda.

'Tell me all about her!'

I realise that I have to lie now, I have to lie until I'm blue in the face. I think about what they say, that if you lie long enough, people will eventually believe you. So I'll just have to lie for long enough.

I tell her about my girlfriend, I make it up, bluff, fib and lie. I think she knows that I'm lying, but she doesn't say anything. She must know that I'm lying, but it's exactly what she wants to hear, so she says nothing. *Please please please, let me, let me, let me, let me get what I want.*

'When can I meet her?' my mother asks.

'Tomorrow,' I say, thinking to myself that there's no time left. I can say all this and still get away with it. Soon it will be over. Soon she will be gone.

'You can meet her tomorrow, Mother. I'll bring her to see you tomorrow. Go to sleep now. Lie down and go to sleep.'

I look at myself in the mirror, see some grey hairs on my temples, and in my sideburns, almost like the rings in a tree: if you count the grey hairs, you can find out how old I am.

I don't do my quiff as high as I used to. I still have one, but it falls down over my forehead, as there's not enough hair to do it as high as before, not even with gel. Anyway, this isn't the right place to have a great quiff. It's impossible to get your hair to stay up in the rain. *The rain falls hard on this humdrum town.*

I can see from photographs that Morrissey has got older too. His hair is quite short now, but he still has sideburns, and he's started to wear Cox loafers and Gucci coats.

Morrissey is so bloody stylish. He always has been. He has more style than the whole pop industry put together. Some people think that he lost it after The Smiths, but that's just bullshit. He's still got what it takes.

I put on my black suit, a black T-shirt and my NHS glasses. The same glasses that Morrissey is wearing on the gatefold of *Hatful Of Hollow*. I bought them through The Smiths' official fan club. They've probably sold glasses like these to thousands of idiots like me.

But that doesn't matter. For me, they're the same glasses that Morrissey used to wear, and they really suit me. What's more, I see less when I put them on, the world becomes hazy and blurred, like sitting inside a car when it's raining so heavily that the windscreen wipers can't keep the front screen clear.

I go into my mother. She's awake now. I've asked the neighbour to come round and look after her, the fat one they call the Princess of Burundi. My mother might need a princess now. While I'm out, the two of them can gossip about Diana and the future of the British royal family.

'Mother,' I say. 'I'm going to get my girlfriend.'

She nods and coughs.

'I'll be back soon,' I say.

It's a warm and humid day. The light is turning from

golden to white. It's been one of those summers with lots of rain. People have complained like children, but I like the rain. I like rain and hopeless politicians. Then at least you've got some opposition. You need something to rail against, something to despise, something to hate, otherwise everything seems pointless.

I climb onto my mother's bike and cycle into town. Where on earth should I look? *Come out and find the one that you love and who loves you.* It's not that bloody easy.

I swing down towards the quay and almost get knocked down by a car; I can hardly see anything with my Morrissey glasses on. It's as if I'm cycling in the middle of the video for 'There Is A Light That Never Goes Out.' Everything is hazy, misty and unclear. Everything is flickering and hopping and jumping. I can't see a bloody thing with these glasses on.

But that's the good thing about them. I used to wear them all the time when I was delivering post. Then I didn't need to see this ugly town, Odda. I have an inner picture of Odda, and it's a beautiful Odda, a dirty and rusty and old Odda, but a beautiful Odda all the same. I don't want to see the other Odda, the new Odda that is trying to be Not-Odda.

Where should I look? What are my chances? How many people live in Odda? Eight thousand? Eight thousand corpses. In the seventies, the council decided that there would be ten thousand 'Oddingers' living here by the year 2000. But the population has just continued to fall. What an utterly ridiculous resolution. Who would want to live here, given the choice? Ten thousand corpses by the year 2000? Ridiculous.

I cycle to the bus station. Maybe I'll meet a girl who doesn't come from Odda. Someone with an open mind, who doesn't know who I am. I lock up the ladies' bike, go in and buy myself a bottle of pop from the kiosk.

Shit, it's like being sixteen again. Sixteen, clumsy and shy. I've always been shy and distant. I have always been criminally shy. I have always been everything that girls don't like. *And time is against me now, and there's no one left to blame.*

I take a drink and think about what I might say. What on earth am I going to say? How can I explain everything in only a few sentences?

A girl gets off the bus and plonks herself down at one of the tables. I study her over the top of my glasses. She looks like she might fit the bill, she looks like a Marita. She has long red hair and no doubt comes from along the fjord. She looks like she's picked lots of apples. I could go straight over to her and ask.

Ask what, though?

I don't know, but I've got nothing to lose. I'm not doing this for myself, I'm doing it for my mother. I straighten my jacket and go over to her table. I want to say something, but I can't get the words out.

I stand there, drinking my pop. I can't get a word out.

Eventually she stands up and asks if I want to sit down. Then she leaves. Walks out of my life. *Oh, please, fulfil me, otherwise, kill me.*

I had a girlfriend when I was nineteen. Suddenly we were standing outside her door – I remember it was snowing. It was a night in February, and everyone else had disappeared all at once, and it was just us, me and her and the snow. We went into her bedsit, and I talked maniacally about Oscar Wilde.

I talked about fat, old Oscar and his books and how witty he was at his wittiest and how much I liked Oscar, and when she finally had had enough of me wittering on about Oscar Wilde, she pulled me to her and kissed me.

And I kissed her. And I wanted to marry her there and then, I wanted to kiss her for the rest of my life; I wanted to lie there on the sofa for the rest of my life. She was so beautiful, she was so soft. But she misunderstood everything. She thought I wanted to sleep with her, and that was all. She thought that was all I wanted to do, to sleep with her. *But I don't want a lover, I just want to be tied to the back of your car, to be tied to the back of your car.*

Another woman comes into the bus station. She's a bit older, maybe around 35 or something like that. She's carrying several plastic bags and has fair hair. It is her. I am ready now, I straighten my glasses and run my fingers through my hair. I am Reggie Kray – I am the last of the famous international playboys. God, I walk like hero; I am a ladies' man – I am *this charming man.*

'Can I sit down here?' I ask. She has bought herself a hot dog. God, I think, she's bought a hot dog, and she's disgusting. How can people stuff themselves with sausages like that? But I think she nods, so I sit down.

I cough and stammer, say something, without quite knowing what I'm saying. Get it wrong from the start, of course. I don't know what I'm saying. It all just falls out of my mouth, like I'm a bag of sweets with a hole in it – everything just falls out, in no particular order.

'What is it you actually want?' the woman asks, with her mouth full of sausage.

'I want you to come home with me,' I say.

Then she stands up and shouts: 'You want me to go home with you?'

I nod.

'Please don't misunderstand,' I say. 'I can pay you.'

Because of my glasses, I don't see her hand until it's too late, but I feel it strike my cheek. An open hand and it stings like hell.

'You pig!' the woman screams, standing up and grabbing her plastic bags.

Everyone looks at me. I don't look up, but I know that everyone is looking at me. I've got my glasses on which means that I can't see, but that doesn't matter, they can obviously still see *me*.

There is complete silence in the waiting room. I sit there with my fizzy drink as if nothing has happened. Nothing has happened, I am completely calm, nothing has happened. I only wish that the ground would open up and take me down.

I wonder whether I should get up and shout: *Listen to me, all of you! I declare, here and now, that life is simply taking and not giving.*

I think to myself that I can cycle back home to my mother and say that my girlfriend couldn't come, that she had to go to work or to the doctor or something; she had a minor stroke, she's been stung by a bee, she can't face it, she's in a coma, she was attacked by a herd of drug-crazed wild Oddingers.

But that would finish my mother. I know that would kill her. I think that I haven't done a single thing in my whole life to make my mother happy. Not one single thing.

'Is anyone sitting here?'

I look up and see the outline of a person. I don't care, I say they can sit down.

I'm a complete fruitcake. Come have a look, everyone, come and see the complete fruitcake, today's main attraction: *the human fruitcake*! The complete fruitcake from Odda!

'What's up with you?' the person asks.

I don't answer. I feel like I'm about to start crying. I have let my mother down, the only person who cares about me.

'Are you stuck in the ice age, or what?' asks the person who has sat down at the table.

I finish my drink and stare out of the window. It's a beautiful day, with clear air and sunshine, but I can't see anything. Everything is blurred. Everything is hazy.

Morrissey said something about happiness. He said that happiness isn't just one thing. Happiness can be eating an ice-cream. Happiness can be Bernard Manning. Happiness can be an old woman falling off a donkey.

I don't know, for Christ's sake, I don't know. I'm too sensitive. I wasn't made for this world. I explode if anyone so much as touches me. *I could have been wild and I could have been free, but Nature played this trick on me.*

'It can't be that bad,' I hear from the other side of the table.

I look at her over the top of my glasses. She has dark blonde hair which is cut straight at the neck. She has a nice shaped face and a big mouth. Beside her is a worn, black suitcase. She's drinking coffee.

'My mother's going to die,' I say.

She puts down her coffee and says that she's sorry to hear that. She didn't mean to upset me.

'That's OK,' I say.

She asks if my mother is in hospital. I tell her that my mother is lying at home in the Beehive and is going to die.

'Why aren't you with her?' the girl asks.

I reply that it's a long story. She says that she has a couple of hours to wait until her bus goes, so she has time to listen.

I look at her and see that she looks like the girl who danced in The Smiths' video for 'How Soon Is Now?' She has the same features as the girl in the video. I say that I'm looking for a partner.

'Who isn't?' the girl says and laughs.

I like her laughter.

I say that my mother has always wanted me to have a girlfriend, but I've spent my life without one. I don't know why I'm saying this to a complete stranger, but I say it.

'I've been without a girlfriend all my life,' I say. 'No girlfriend and no charm.'

'I don't believe you,' she says.

'Fine,' I say.

What am I doing here, I think to myself. This is fucking hopeless. Everything is hopeless. I am hopeless. I've got no charm, all I've got is this shyness. *Sleep on and dream of Love, because it's the closest you will get to love.*

'Will you be my girlfriend?' I ask the girl.

She laughs.

'Don't you think we should take things a bit slower?'

She laughs. I don't like her laughter.

'Sorry,' I say and get up. 'It was just a bad joke.'

I go out to my mother's bike. *Sweetness, sweetness, I was only joking!* I unlock the bike and get ready to go home and kill my mother.

I'm about to cycle back up to the Beehive, go in to my mother and kill her in cold blood.

Mother, I will say, sorry, sorry, sorry. I've been lying to you.

I jump on the bike and am just about to pedal off when I hear someone shouting behind me.

'Hello, wait!'

I turn round. I see a blurred figure running towards me.

'I am so happy to meet you, Marita!' my mother says, clasping the girl's hand in her lap. 'You have no idea how happy it makes me! Now I can die safe in the knowledge that someone is there to look after my boy.'

My mother smiles and squeezes the girl's hand so hard that her knuckles whiten.

'I think you should rest now, Mother,' I say.

I can see on the clock that the girl has to leave soon if she's going to catch her bus.

'Give me a hug!' my mother says to the girl who's supposed to be my girlfriend.

They hug each other. It nearly brings tears to my eyes.

My mother has asked her all sorts of questions, almost like an interrogation, as if the girl had been taken down to the police station and my mother was the kind officer on duty. The girl has answered as well as she could, only looking at me every now and then to see if I nod or shake my head.

She's been amazing, she's made things up and spun tales. For the first time ever, I have made my mother happy. For the first time, I have done something really good for my mother. And I think to myself that it's typical that it's all rubbish.

The girl leans down over my mother and kisses her on the forehead. I see that it makes my mother happy, she closes her eyes and lets out a long, happy sigh.

'I'm so tired,' she says. 'So tired.'

I follow the girl out into the stairwell.

'Thank you,' I say. 'I don't know how to thank you enough.'

She smiles. She takes her hand and tucks her hair back behind her ear. It's an incredibly beautiful movement, pure poetry, if you ask me. I've always liked girls who do just that, lift their hands up to their head and tuck their hair behind their ear.

'You're lucky to have such a lovely mother,' the girl says and looks at me.

Then she takes off my glasses. I actually never use them indoors, but with so much going on, I completely forgot to take them off.

'You're lovely too, you know,' she says and strokes my cheek.

I can see clearly now and I think that the girl really does look like that girl in The Smiths' video. Only she's a bit older. I've always liked the girl in The Smiths' video. I don't know anyone who's as pretty as she is.

'Shall I come down with you?' I ask quickly.

I pick up her suitcase and carry it down the stairs. Out on the pavement I hand her her suitcase and ask if she can remember how to get back to the bus station, as I have to go in to my mother again. She nods.

'Bye,' she says and walks down the road.

I watch her walk away. Halfway down the street she turns.

'You know what?' she shouts to me. 'I like The Smiths too!'

Shit! I never said anything about liking The Smiths to her. She must have seen all my records or the posters in my room.

I think: *Oh God, my chance is finally here!* I have to run after her. I have to stop her. I have to talk to her.

But suddenly it's as if I'm paralysed, a terrible fear comes over me. I could easily run after her, catch up with her and stop her, but I just stay standing where I am.

I remain rooted to the asphalt. I stand there thinking that I forgot to ask what she's called. I see her disappear round the corner by the shop and I realise that I know nothing about her, and now it's too late, soon everything will be too late.

My mother calls to me from inside, she's in pain. I go in with a glass of water for her. Then I see that there is vomit and blood on the floor.

'What is it?' I ask.

'I don't know,' she says.

'Shall I ring the doctor?' I ask.

She answers no. Doctors have shone lights in her and at her, and taken countless pictures. The doctors have perforated her with needles and tubes, they've taken blood tests and ECGs and x-rays. The doctors can't do anything more for her now.

'I'm so happy,' my mother says. 'You've found yourself a lovely girl.'

She lies back against the pillows and closes her eyes. I go to get something to clean up with. Then I sit down in the old wing chair and look out of the window. The light outside is harsh and white, a white overhead light that exposes everything in sight, no one can hide any lies on a day like this.

Except me.

I think about the girl. She was suddenly just there, and just as suddenly she was gone. Now it's as if she had never been here.

This is the day my mother is going to die. The last day in August. The same day that Diana died. Only Diana died at a hundred kilometres an hour. My mother is dying incredibly slowly.

But this is the day. I know it. I can see it on her. She is barely of this world any more. I sit there, in the chair, and know that in a few hours my mother will be gone. Soon she will have gone the whole way. *Sing me to sleep, sing me to sleep, sing me to sleep.*

When she has died, I will cycle down to the flower shop and buy lots of daffodils, which I will scatter all over the room. Around my dead mother, over the bed and over the floor, just like in the video for 'This Charming Man'. And from the other side, my mother will be able to smell this life, the poetry of the flowers, this final greeting from her only son.

And then I will put on my suit and my Morrissey hornrimmed glasses and I will walk, like a blind man, I will walk out into the world, just walk and walk. I will go as far as I must, to find that girl; I don't know where she lives, I don't even know what she's called.

And when I have gone far enough to find her, I will take off my glasses and ask her once again: 'Will you be my girlfriend?'

Translated from the Norwegian by Kari Dickson

She was Singing

Danielle Picard

'Regular as clockwork, the old man,' she thought, when, after one last traffic light, like every day her car went round the bend in an upside-down S on the motorway slip road which skirted an area of communal gardens. 'It's strange that he's out so early. He can't live in the garden shed?' There were indeed homes just at the edge of the gardens. Maybe he lived in one of those buildings? Maybe even in that little house, tiny beside the council flats, which seemed to have valiantly resisted the weather, the so-called social policies and the developers. If he lived in that little house, the next-door garden was its natural extension, it was perfectly normal for the old man to be there early, or that he went for a little walk only to taste the morning air as she would so have liked to do (maybe later on she too would have had a garden where she could taste the weather; maybe the old man had had an active life during which he too would have dreamed of this moment), or that he felt well enough at that time to do a bit of gardening, or for other reasons that were even more obvious or more inconceivable for her: is not every person mysterious and opaque?

So her thoughts went every day when the green gardens, the valiant little house and the venerable old man came up on her right hand side. 'How old would Dad be?'

Every day the calculation was made while she cautiously checked in her rear mirror that the lane was clear for going onto the motorway, then she imagined the happiness her father would have felt in knowing his grand-daughter, now a beautiful thirty-year-old woman. Then only, after the easy calculation whose result she knew perfectly, and this brief but tender thought towards her daughter, she felt sure that her working day was really beginning. She was surprised at singing, amazed at carrying out so many mental activities, but, after all, there were very different areas of the mind.

The short ceremony was coming to an end. The young woman felt she was beyond tears, a hard block of insensitivity. A small crowd had accompanied her mother towards nothingness, close family, friends, strangers, some of whom came to introduce themselves: colleagues of the dead woman, members of associations to which her mother belonged, an old man that she considered senile as he repeated while shaking her hand: 'She was singing, she was singing.'

Before that, the young woman had had to identify her mother's body. An ordeal.

The enquiry into the causes of the accident had begun. What exactly had happened? What were her mother's last moments? A civil case, she could have sight of the copies that her lawyer made from the various statements. A witness said that he had followed with his eyes her mother's Twingo from the last red light and had seen a car going at high speed the wrong way up the motorway slip road, then he had heard a crash, a screech of tyres, the roar of engines starting up again, and another crash, but he had not been able to see the collision itself, hidden by a thicket, and under his eyes there was no car any more. He wondered where the car going the wrong way had gone. He had run, but not very fast – it was his heart – and had with horror recognised the woman's car; he had taken some time to dare to go near and call useless emergency services from his mobile. He gave other superfluous details. Very upset, the young woman realised that this man was the last person to have seen her mother alive, apart from her killer – but had the latter seen her at all? Immediately, feeling nervous, she decided to meet this witness of those last moments.

He lived, at a few tens of metres from the last traffic light before the motorway slip road, in a delightful little house at the foot of quiet council flats, at the edge of gardens whose peacefulness did not seem to be affected by the low density traffic. To her great surprise, the noise of the motorway seemed to her to be softened, while she had imagined it would be unbearable; she noticed a protective wall, broken for the slip road to pass through. The old man asked her to come in. He spoke to her about this woman who was her mother, told her that she shared his life for some months, from the day he had noticed that she always went by at the same time. He was pleased when the lights were red, as then he could, for a bit longer, see her and above all, hear her.

'Hear her?'

'Yes. Mind you, only in spring and in summer when it was fine.'

'What did you hear?'

'Well, she used to sing. She was – and even when the car windows were closed and I couldn't hear her – my ray of sunshine for the whole day. Sometimes – I suppose that then she wasn't going to her work, I suppose that she practised a profession – I didn't see her for a few days and even a few weeks, and it was as if I were suddenly a widower, forgive me.'

'You knew her? You were...'

'No, no, no, don't believe that...We never spoke to each other, we never met. Maybe she didn't even know I existed. I don't think that she ever noticed me. You know, she was driving. She drove well, she didn't look at the landscape. I was part of the landscape. Sometimes, at the red light, she looked to the right, to the left. But would she have noticed an old fool in his garden first thing in the morning, who was looking, not at his flowers and his vegetables, but at a young woman at the wheel? Forgive me, your mother looked very young, to me. Enamoured with a young woman driving along... I must seem ridiculous to you.'

'No, no, no,' she protested.

'She would sing. Often even at the top of her voice. I used to hear her when her windows were open at the red light. Besides, it's because she sang that I noticed her, one morning when, as I like to do since I've been able to acquire the garden just beside my home, from the council – without pulling strings, I assure you – one morning when I had gone to taste the air, that's my expression. I heard a truly resonant voice, deliciously unaffected. I thought about Ulysses' sirens, the Lorelei... but kind...'

He hesitated on the edge of the explanation. The young woman indicated to him that she had understood.

'On the day... that day, was she singing?'

He nodded yes. With a lump in her throat, she left without saying a word. This stranger knew more than she did about her mother, knew a facet of her that was not known by her daughter. But indignation rumbled on inside her. She was sure she had never heard her mother sing. Although, maybe, when she was small, otherwise from where, from whom did she know those lullabies, those nursery rhymes, those children's songs that she didn't remember having learnt and that she herself had sung to her own daughter?

Later on, on any old excuse, she rang her sister.

'By the way, it's just come to me, Mum, she sang?'

'What do you mean, she sang? I... Why? I don't know. No, I... It's stupid. Now that you... I don't remember having heard her sing. Maybe when I was small... I know some children's songs. It must have been her who...'

'Leave it, it doesn't matter...'

The young woman asked the other members of her

family the same thing. She asked her mother's friends if, among her extra-professional activities, her mother was a member of a gym club for example, or of a choir where she sang...

'Sing? No...I don't think I ever heard her sing. But that doesn't mean that she was gloomy or dull. On the contrary, your mother was quite cheerful, smiling...'

They all confirmed what she knew, what she was sure of: her mother didn't sing. The old man was maybe a bit deranged, or had too much imagination. He heard a siren when there was only a woman...A woman. Her mother. Not a siren, but kind.

When she got back to the hotel, she read the copy of another statement: the evidence of a lorry-driver. At the red light, he was at the side of the Twingo. His fully-loaded lorry had stopped very slowly. That's why he had not been present at the accident, strictly speaking. As soon as he saw the car overturned, he had stopped his HGV; he had had a vague impression of another car being present in the area and of an old man with a telephone, but, above all, he had been struck by the silence – the traffic was not dense at that time. And by the music of the car stereo.

The young woman raised her head. That was the comforting explanation: the old man, from the music, had built up a scaffolding in which it was the *woman* who was singing. Yes, of course, her mother often listened to music. She felt the absolute necessity of knowing the last sounds that her mother had heard.

The old man, when questioned again by her, described too the impressive silence after the violence of the two impacts and immediately becoming aware of lively music coming out of this crashed car in which the woman was left, in what state, his mind refused to imagine. He had had found it difficult, he said, to make these twisted sheets of metal coincide with the image of the woman who, a moment before, was singing.

'She was singing along with the music of the car stereo?'

'No, no, no. At the red light, she was singing. Alone. At the top of her voice.'

'She never used to sing, all her close family will tell you.'

'And me, I'm telling you that she was always singing.'

'The lorry driver said that he heard music.'

'So did I! Maybe after she stopped, she put on her stereo? Maybe one of the impacts switched the stereo on?'

He was puzzled too. Upon seeing him doubt, search for an explanation, she no longer wanted to see him as senile.

'This lorry was beside her, at the red light. It would be enough for you...'

She understood immediately. Meet the lorry-driver. He was at the other end of France, his wife said, he would be back tomorrow evening. At the hotel, she plucked up all her courage to open at last the bag that the police had given her which held the objects taken from the car as samples for forensic examination, having been placed under seal. A scarf, the handbag that her sister had given to their mother the year before, CDs... The choice was eclectic, she recognised her mother's personality there with a smile. She was struck, however, not to find any discs of classical music. It was strange for someone who listened to it a great deal. The young woman mused that she herself didn't like listening to classical music in the car, or else it would have had to be in a perfectly soundproofed luxury car, with an excellent car stereo...Maybe her mother, too...

The next morning, the telephone rang; her lawyer told her that the reckless driver had been found, that he had confessed, that the prosecutor had taken the seals off the car. She decided, while waiting for the lorry-driver to come home, to go to see her mother's last home at the garage. In order to worry? In order to hurt herself? To know? To know what?

The front left door had disappeared, but the key was in the ignition. She did not dare slide over the seat where her

SHE WAS SINGING

mother had faced death. For a long time, she stayed there, not knowing how to place herself between all this tangible material and the unreality that constituted her mother's death. She was caught up with an enquiry that suddenly seemed absurd to her, but that a moment before she had regarded as necessary: music or singing? What music or which song? She felt she could only picture her mother's death after having rid herself of this obsession, a screen, which she knew was temporary, which was strained between two incompatible realities: her mother always alive for her, her mother dead. The music or the song? What music or which song? The dilemma seemed to contain the key to this death.

The car stereo! Why had she not thought about it before? That's what knows the answer! Does it still work? A sacrilegious finger reaches towards one of the buttons. At the same time, a CD comes out of the unit. Bach. The last sounds to reach her mother's living ears?

She stretches out another sacrilegious finger towards another button. Music bursts out. Nostalgia, the screen says. Did her mother sing? Did she listen? Bach or Nostalgia? Something else? Who switched off the stereo? When? Did it go on working after its listener's life had ended, the only echo of her listening beyond her passing? The car stereo will not speak.

Upon the lorry-driver's return, she decided to continue her search, without believing in the possibility of answer. At the red light, for sure, with the noise of an HGV engine against a voice of a living woman or that of a car stereo, the man could not have heard anything.

He had heard. She was singing.

'What? What was she singing?' Her vehemence surprised the lorry-driver. 'You must know, they were her last words, I want to know. It would be a message for me. Please try, remember, I'm begging you...'

'It was something that I didn't know.'

'Opera?'
'No, something more modern, rhythmic – I think.'
'A variety song?
He didn't know. He was sorry. He couldn't help her.
She thought about the old man. Could he have identified this tune that he said he heard? His voice, his elocution, his home showed he was an educated man. He wasn't at home.

Devastated, she decided, before leaving town to go home, to go and face, after the enclosed space, intimate and impersonal at once, of the car, the place of the accident – of the murder. A more open space than the inflexible sequence of time unfolded through sounds and words.

It was morning, maybe around the time when her mother passed along here... She went through the bushes that had hidden the accident from the old man's view. He was there, looking at an area where the grass was scorched. He raised his eyes as she came near.

'She was singing. At the top of her voice.'
She didn't want to know any more.

Translated from the French by Felicity McNab

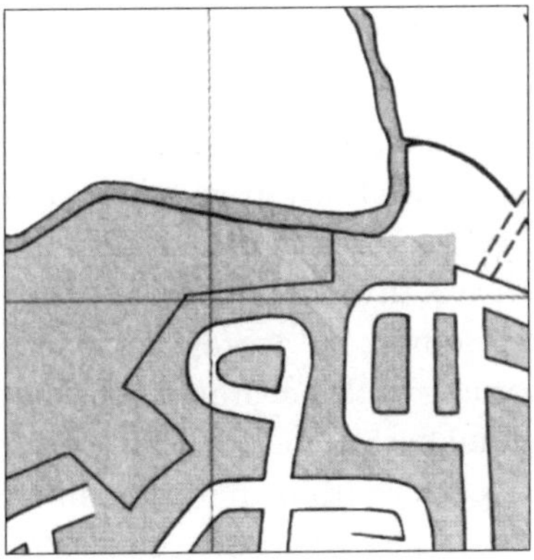

Żurek Soup

Olga Tokarczuk

'We should have brought the pram,' said one woman to the other once they were on the road to the bus stop, which hadn't been snow-ploughed for ages.

The older one was carrying the child wrapped in a blanket that now, in the rapidly falling dusk, looked grey as if it was dirty. The younger one walked behind her mother, treading in her footprints in the snow – it was easier like that.

'We should have gone in daylight, not at night,' the older woman spoke again.

'Should have, should have,' said the younger. 'I wasn't ready.'

'There was no need to get dressed up like that.'

'You were getting dressed up too.'

'No I wasn't. I couldn't find my hat.'

They only just caught the bus. It arrived steamed up and almost empty – like a blown egg made of metal. There was a gang of teenagers squashed into the back seat. They must have been off to town for the disco. The younger woman kept staring at them furtively, but avidly. She was eyeing up the girls, especially the one in a leather jacket and tight jeans. Her mother softly asked her a question, but she just snarled in reply. Then she wiped the steamed-up window and gazed into the gloom outside, where lights were twinkling. The young people travelled onwards, but the two women got out at the next stop, where a side road joined the dual carriageway, along which some big lorries went roaring by.

They passed a festively illuminated motel and reached the fish and chip shop. They stopped for a moment in front of a sign saying 'Always Coca-Cola', which lit up the façade of the newly renovated house like a vast red moon.

'Shall we call him out here, or how are we going to do it?' asked the mother.

'You go, I'll wait here with the child.'

The older woman went inside and came back soon after.

'He's not there. He's at home.'

They gave each other a quick glance and headed into the yard.

A dog tied to its kennel started barking. A light came on automatically. The snow had mercifully covered all the construction yard clutter – stacks of planks, packs of Styrofoam wrapped in plastic and pyramids of hollow bricks. Władysław was building a garage.

He came out to meet them. A well-built gingery man in a knitted sweater with sleeves that were unravelling relentlessly, he stared at them in amazement.

'What are you doing here at this time of day?' he asked without saying hello.

'We've got business to discuss,' said the older woman.

'Really?' he drawled, even more amazed.

'Can we come in?'

He hesitated, but only for a second, almost imperceptibly. He let them inside, into a freshly plastered hall where small lumps of cement crunched under their shoes. They went into a messy kitchen. He must have been tinkering with some part of the sink, because the cupboard had been detached from the wall, revealing the mysteries of pipes and U-bends.

'Can we sit down?' asked the older woman.

ŻUREK SOUP

He set out two chairs for them, almost in the very middle of the kitchen, lit himself a cigarette and leaned against the dismounted cupboard. Only now did he see the child, and smiled.

'A boy or a girl?'

'A boy, a boy,' replied the younger woman and unwrapped the child from the blanket.

She pushed the woolly blue bonnet off his eyes. The child was asleep. His wrinkled little face reminded Władysław of a freshly shelled hazelnut. It was ugly.

'Lovely,' he said. 'What's his name?'

'He hasn't got one yet,' said the younger woman gaily.

'Władysław,' the older one was quick to offer.

'Władysław?' he said in amazement. 'Who calls a child Władysław these days?'

He scowled and dragged on his cigarette.

'Your name is Władysław, and so's his...' the older woman continued.

'Maybe it is – who said it's not?'

There was a silence. The man flicked ash onto the floor.

'Well then?'

The woman averted her gaze towards the tip of a curtain rod that was leaning against the wall and said in that direction: 'It's your child, Władysław. The holidays are coming, so we want to christen him.'

The man's face hardened.

'You must be fucking crazy, Halina. How can it be my child? Come on, Iwonka,' he said, turning to the girl, 'how can it be my child? What are you two on about?'

Iwonka chewed her lip and began to rock the child rapidly. It woke up and had a short cry.

'Who is the father?' he asked.

'You are. It's your child.'

The man stood up and stubbed the cigarette out on his shoe.

'That's enough. Get out of here, both of you.'

They got up reluctantly. Iwonka pulled the baby's little blue bonnet over his eyes.

'Come on, come on,' he chivvied them.

'All right, Władysław, in that case the father is your son Jacek,' said the mother suddenly in the doorway without turning round.

'He was here for Easter,' added Iwonka truculently.

'Get lost.'

The door closed behind them. They stood in silence on the dirty, trodden snow. After a while the light went out.

'Now what?' Iwonka asked her mother.

'What do you think? Nothing.'

The bus wasn't due for an hour, so they headed home on foot.

'I told you to bring the pram. Now it'll take us at least an hour.'

'Better walk than wait at the bus stop and get frozen.'

That night the child was restless. Iwonka slept like the dead, so her mother wetted the corner of a nappy in warm water and gave it to the baby to suck. His little lips began to squirm. Firelight flickered through chinks in the kitchen range.

Next morning both women were in the shop. Iwonka bought herself a Magnum ice cream. It cost a fortune. Her mother reproached her, saying it wasn't even the money, but that she'd catch cold and lose her breast milk. Iwonka calmly ate the ice cream and shrugged. The child was asleep in a bright blue pram.

'What a pretty little chap,' the shop lady gushed; she had come onto the steps outside wearing a non-iron white overall on top of her sweater. 'Oh, how cold it is!'

Soon a queue had formed in the shop, as was usually the case around noon. This time it wasn't just the local men coming in for cheap wine or people driving through wanting cola and nuts for the journey to the border. Today the

ŻUREK SOUP

housewives had come for cake flavourings, vanilla sugar, margarine and raisins. With as much care as a pharmacist, the shop lady was weighing out marshmallows, chocolate-coated jellies and special Christmas sweets, where what counted most were the shiny gold and purple wrappers – these little beauties were to hang on the Christmas tree. The customers weren't at all concerned about the queue moving quickly, far from it – as soon as they took their turn at the counter, each of them chatted with the shop lady, who would abandon her columns of figures and little bags of baking powder, lean on the counter and listen to the tales they had brought. It even looked as if they weren't using money to pay, as if the money were just ritual pebbles. For raisins, baking powder and cheap wine you paid with a little story, a question or some witty repartee. That was why it was taking so long.

A smart dark green car stopped outside the shop, one of those very new ones with a high, box-shaped back. There were skis on the roof. A man got out of the car, wearing a fleece, Gore-Tex gloves and a funny cap. He said something to a woman who stayed in the car with two teenage children, then skipped into the shop and took his place at the end of the queue, right behind Matuszek.

'Got any żurek soup?' asked the fleecy fellow, rubbing his hands, and added inconsequentially: 'Brrr, it's cold.'

This question about żurek soup soured the chatty atmosphere. Called to order in mid-monologue, the shop lady glanced round at the newcomer.

'Żurek soup, the kind in bottles. Or it could be in a jar – I don't know what kind you usually have, the bottles or the jars.'

'Żurek soup,' said Mrs Matwiejuk, prompting the shop lady as she began to pack her small purchases into a plastic bag.

Everyone cast a discreet glance at the visitor. The snow was melting on his brightly coloured, trendy snow boots. The yellow label on his sky-blue jacket announced some garish truth in a foreign language. The shop lady glanced at the bottom shelf.

'There is some,' she said. 'The last bottle.'

'So it's in bottles. Where we are, up north, we've got żurek soup in jars,' explained the man, looking around cheerfully at the customers' faces. 'We're on a skiing trip to Austria for the holidays and my wife insisted we must have żurek soup, and this is the last shop before the border,' he said, more quietly now, addressing himself for some unknown reason to Matuszek.

Matuszek turned his head away and gazed calmly at the cigarette brands on display in a glass case. The queue moved forward one place in silence as Mrs Matwiejuk stood counting her change by the door.

'What's Christmas without żurek soup?' the man spoke again. His high, ringing, confident voice had a wounding effect on the ears. 'It's our Polish speciality. I've been in lots of countries in Europe and all over the world, but they never have żurek soup. So I thought, as I was driving along, if I don't buy it here, I won't get it anywhere. They don't have żurek soup in the Czech Republic.'

No one answered. The man began to stamp his feet and blow on his hands. Confused by the presence of a stranger, the shop lady, that talkative shop lady, was doing her job efficiently and thoroughly. The queue was moving forward quickly, too quickly, because no one was in a hurry.

'It's cold,' said the stranger to Matuszek, rubbing his hands together again in a theatrical way.

Matuszek glanced at him and gave the faintest flicker of a smile out of politeness, then turned to face the cigarettes in the display case again.

'We've got an apartment booked in the Alps. My God, they've got great ski lifts there – what a place. It takes an hour or even better to come down. And there's a bar and a pool in the hotel at the bottom. We do our own meals. There's a kitchen in every apartment, so my wife'll be able to heat up the żurek soup. And I'll take a bit of sausage too, but a good one, mind. Have they got good sausage here?' he asked, suddenly sounding concerned.

The next woman reluctantly moved away from the counter. The shop lady unzipped her sweater at the neck.

'I can see there is some, but sausage that only costs six zlotys can't be any good,' said the man.

A car horn sounded. The man went over to the door and let a swirling cloud of frozen air into the shop. He shouted something in the direction of the car and came back to his place in line.

'The woman's fretting because we're supposed to be in the Alps by evening. But I felt like a bit of żurek soup.'

Matuszek bought some cigarettes, some orange essence, a half litre of vodka and some bread. The shop lady efficiently added up the column of figures and wrapped the bottle in the bill.

'And some żurek soup,' he said. 'A bottle of żurek soup.'

The whole shop went extremely quiet. The shop lady solemnly passed him the bottle. Matuszek quickly paid.

'Hey, mister...' the man in the fleece began, totally astonished, but in an instant Matuszek had picked up his shopping and left.

Outside the shop he saw Halina and her not-quite-all-there daughter, and handed her the bottle.

'Take it. We don't eat żurek soup – we prefer beetroot,' he said, and told her to drop in that evening for a long promised quilt.

Iwonka was too shy to go in. She stood by the fence with her teeth chattering, goodness knows whether from cold or fear.

'What are you afraid of, you ninny? They're not going to eat you. You should have been afraid then, not now,' her mother told her.

'There are some men in there. You go, I'll wait here with the baby.'

'It's a good thing they are – maybe now we'll manage to get something sorted. In front of witnesses. Come on!'

The girl followed her reluctantly.

Four men were sitting at the kitchen table. Matuszek had just poured the last round. His wife, big and stout, was bustling about straining the milk. A yeast cake with crumble topping was cooling on the sideboard. It was nice and warm.

'Mother, the girls have come for the eiderdown,' said Matuszek.

He drew up the one empty chair for them. Halina sat down on the edge of it, while Iwonka stood by the door with the child.

'Well, cheers,' said Góral and knocked back his glass. Without a word the others did the same, cleared their throats and drank some orangeade.

Mrs Matuszek left the room and came straight back with a bundle wrapped in plastic and tied with string. She cooed at the child.

'What's his name?'

'He hasn't got one yet,' Halina was quick to reply.

Iwonka started shuffling nervously on the spot.

'When's the christening?'

Halina shrugged.

'That's a decent quilt,' said Mrs Matuszek. 'Aired all summer in the attic. Have you got a cover?'

'He's the father,' Iwonka suddenly blurted sombrely, nodding at Góral.

There was an awkward silence.

'Well, Iwonka?' her mother encouraged her.

'You're the father,' said the girl, looking him straight in the eye now.

Mrs Matuszek lifted the baby's bonnet from his brow and took a close look at him.

'I've got my four,' said Góral at last. 'Leave me in peace, girl, you haven't a clue who you've slept with.'

ŻUREK SOUP

'Well!' said Halina ominously.

'I've slept with her,' shouted Kawka.

His speech was slurred and his eyes were shining drunkenly. The fellow hadn't a head for drink.

'Yes, I've slept with her,' he repeated slowly. 'But I s-l-e-p-t; I was so drunk I went out like a light, so it wasn't me.'

'She's already been to Władysław's and tried to pin it on him. Who knows whose child it is...'

'A child is a child,' said Mrs Matuszek.

'She was carrying on with a soldier from the watchtower. Everyone saw them,' added Góral. 'Like looking for a needle in a haystack.'

He got up, took his cap from the peg and moved towards the door.

'My God,' groaned Mrs Matuszek. 'Why didn't you keep an eye on her? Halina, it's your fault, it's your fault.'

'Is that what you think? What was I supposed to do? Tie her up by the leg? I'd like to know how you'd have managed. She's a child in the body of a mature woman.'

'Jerzyk?' said Mrs Matuszek suddenly full of suspicion, turning to the youngest man, her nephew.

Góral stopped in the doorway.

Jerzyk blushed to the tips of his ears, making his piercingly blue highlander's eyes appear to light up.

'It wasn't me, Auntie, I was careful.'

Kawka broke into a fitful cackle.

'It'll take at least half a litre to get that one sorted. Well, Mrs Matuszek, time to put out more drink.'

Mrs Matuszek stood helplessly in the middle of the kitchen looking now at Jerzyk, now at Góral, now at her husband. She seemed even fatter now, as heavy as a piece of furniture. Everyone was waiting for her to say something, and her lips were twitching, as if trying to form the shape of a special term to cover everything at once, from start to finish. But plainly she couldn't do it, because she went up to the table, slapped her hand on the oilcloth surface and said:

'That's enough drinking. Go now, tomorrow's Christmas Eve, you've work to do at home.'

She grabbed the bundle and thrust it into Halina's arms. Halina embraced it like a monstrous great baby nest, buried her face in the plastic and burst into tears. Mrs Matuszek began feverishly clearing the table. Without a word the guests got up and headed for the door.

Just then her husband spoke up.

'Wait a moment, wait a moment,' he said. 'Hold on.'

He stopped talking, as if he was still thinking, as if he was trying to make a decision, and drummed his fingers on the table.

'I am the baby's father.'

There was a long silence. There he sat; his wife went on standing in the middle of the kitchen while everyone else remained crowded in the doorway in a puddle of melted snow. Then Mrs Matuszek screamed at the top of her voice: 'Have you gone mad? You can't have children. We haven't had a child in twenty years and everyone knows you can't have children because you had an accident.'

'Be quiet, woman. Shut up. It's my child.'

Kawka staggered over to a chair and sat down.

'All right, then. As that's the case, you'd better put out more drink...'

Shifting from foot to foot, Iwonka was nonchalantly rocking the baby.

'But you can't...' Mrs Matuszek started up again, as her plump hands found the hem of her apron and pressed it to her eyes. Then she ran out, slamming the door.

Matuszek reached over to the sideboard and fetched out a bottle. He took the glasses from the sink and poured six shots of vodka.

'She won't,' said Halina, pointing at Iwonka. 'She's not eighteen yet. And she's breast-feeding.'

They drank up in solemn silence.

'So when's the christening?' asked Matuszek.

ŻUREK SOUP

'The priest said it could be around New Year.'

'Then here's to the christening around New Year,' mumbled Kawka and emptied his glass before anyone else.

Then Matuszek told them all to go home. He said tomorrow was Christmas Eve and they had work to do. In the doorway Halina wiped her tears on her sleeve and smiled at Matuszek.

'Thank you for the żurek soup,' she said.

They walked home across country, over pure, virgin snow, Iwonka treading in her mother's footprints.

Translated from the Polish by Antonia Lloyd-Jones

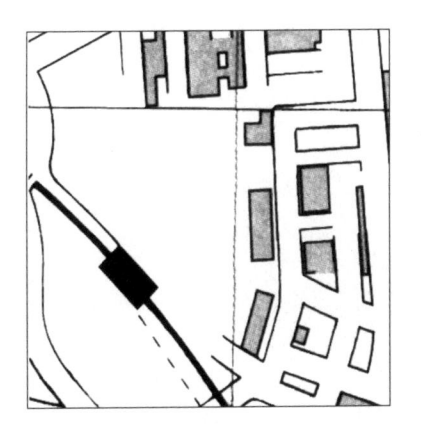

Fog Island

Mehmet Zaman Saçlıoğlu

The train was moving fast. Only two of us remained in the compartment as the others got off at the previous station. My travelling companion, a slim, light brown haired man in his thirties, a little younger than I, took off his shoes and stretched out to sleep on the seat opposite. I was considering doing the same but hesitated, as there were only fifteen or twenty minutes left before my stop.

    I moved next to the window and pressed my nose against the glass as if hoping to see something through the pitch dark. No moon, no stars, no lights to be seen out there. My eyelids became heavy, lulled by the constant rattling and swaying of the train. Just as I closed my eyes I noticed that the train sounds had changed and the shaking stopped. The train was slowing down. Soon it came to a halt. Outside, there was nothing to be seen. I entered the aisle and peered out but still nothing. This was no ordinary darkness.

    I pulled down the window and detected there was movement outside. This strange darkness – like a curious child who sticks his finger into every hole he can reach – flowed through the window, twisting, winding, becoming white. Then I realised we were in the midst of a dense fog. For a moment a light shone through the moving mist. I was never aware that this last train of the day made such a stop. I closed the window to those foggy fingers. As I was about to return to my compartment, the door to the car at the other end of the aisle opened and the conductor entered ringing a small bell:

'Breakdown! We'll be here for an hour. Please do not get off the train, the fog is very thick....'

As he passed by me I asked the conductor the name of this place.

'Second Island station,' he said.

I said I'd never heard of it before.

'This is a very small station,' he said. 'Not every train stops here.'

My travelling companion also awoke and was putting on his shoes. He approached me with sleepy eyes, touched my arm and cocked his head as if to ask what was happening. A questioning sound came from his mouth. I realized that he was mute, and it occurred to me that he might also be deaf.

'Breakdown,' I said slowly so he could read my lips.

I was not mistaken. My travelling companion was both mute and deaf – but we found a way of communicating. His face lightened up as he noticed the fog. He opened the window, stretched out his arm and waved it in the fog while uttering joyous sounds. Then he turned to me and made a sign with his hand for me to follow him outside. His finger pointing to the outside, he opened the door, then grasping the iron handle, stepped down. He was emitting little screams and laughing. As he reached the ground he let go, turned around and extended his hands toward me.

The view was so extraordinary yet frightening. My companion's outstretched hands, his face and a part of his upper body were still visible, but the lower part of his body was fading away and the feet had already disappeared into the fog. I moved my lips expressively, saying, 'Don't walk too far, you'll get lost.' He shook his head, not understanding my plea. 'Don't go ... the fog,' I said slowly mouthing every word.

He waved his hand as if to say that it didn't matter and with raised eyebrow and shoulder, pointed to the train. I guessed he meant that the train was safely beside us.

Not to leave him alone and exposed to every kind of accident that might occur in the fog since he could not hear, I stepped off the train.

I could hardly see my own feet. Like a child about to swim and who cannot separate his hands from the pier when attempting the deep water for the first time, I held tightly to the iron handle of the train. After some hesitation, I let go and stepped next to my friend whose face was barely visible. My breathing was constricted.

'Eternity,' I said, forgetting he was deaf. I whispered to myself this time, 'It's like eternity.'

This surprised me, that the thick fog that hindered my view would evoke a feeling of eternity. I thought of the friend next to me. Was it the same for him? Did he constantly feel himself in an eternity of silence? We were standing about two metres apart. I could see him but as I took one step back his vision would fade away. My friend moved his arms up and down, the fog flowing in small clouds between his fingers, under his arms. Just as he was about to stand still, he would begin his arm movements again. In the course of this game he was uttering jubilant sounds. I failed to notice that we had gradually changed our position ten, maybe more, steps away from the train until I saw a look of amazement on his face, then fear. He whirled around a couple of times, then turned to me with questioning eyes. The train was out of sight. My friend approached me and took my hand, his voice making sounds of questioning and fear now. I held his shoulders, spelling out slowly so that he could read my lips, 'Don't be afraid, the train didn't go... it's still here!'

He nodded his head as if he understood. We took a few steps hand in hand, but the train was not in that direction. We stopped. His hand in mine felt like that of a helpless child. I turned to him, put my finger to my lips for him to be quiet. I didn't want to miss any sounds coming from the train. But neither voice nor light came from that great mass nearby.

Silence stretched out as if rushing all around us, as if the fog were grinding down all sounds into sameness.

I remembered the story about the Trojan King Tithanos who grew smaller and smaller while getting older and, at the end, turned into a cricket, a mere sound. Still I could hear nothing. After a couple of minutes I could not stand the silence and shouted, 'Hello! You people on the train!' But no reply. 'Mr. Conductor, can you hear me?' But the silence was unbroken.

My friend noticed that I was shouting and began his wordless calls. Instinctively, not consciously, I understood what he was saying: 'We are lost, help us, where are you? I am scared, come here!' My deaf mute friend had placed so much feeling into this strange screaming with words that can't be found in any dictionary. He shouted twice, then began looking at my face to learn if any answer was received.

I was all ears. After a couple of seconds, I heard a weak voice. Seeing that I had raised my head and turned in the direction of the voice, my friend again shouted. I made him hush. He was agitated. He also took a position as if to listen, his eyes fastened on my face trying to catch any reflection of any sound I might hear.

I believed I heard that weak voice again and made a sign to my friend to keep quiet. He nodded as if to say he would. The weak voice was coming closer, whatever it was. I heard a scraping and tapping sound. Hearing it better I shouted, 'Hello, who is there?'

The voice stopped. I was afraid that somebody or something would come and hit my deaf friend. I became anxious and called out again: 'Hello, here we are. We lost the train!'

The voice started again but I couldn't gauge the distance. I looked in the direction it was coming from without seeing a thing. Suddenly someone called out, 'Yes, where are you?'

I relaxed. 'Here,' I said, 'we are here.'

My friend also understood that I was talking to someone and expected an explanation. I made a sign to him to wait a little bit. The smile on my face calmed him down.

'Stay where you are and call to me. I am coming toward you,' said the voice. 'Keep on talking so that I may find you. How many of you are out there?'

'Two,' I said, 'We are two people.'

'What is the colour of your clothes?'

'Our clothes? What are you going to do with our clothes? We cannot even see the tips of our noses.'

'I mean, I am just asking for fun. I cannot repeat all the time, where are you, to the right or the left? Are you going to say to me like a car park attendant, "go left, go right?" Just say something so that I can find you.'

'My friend has a pink bikini and I am wearing long white underwear.'

'My God, you really are lost!'

Meanwhile the voice had come quite close to us. We saw his silhouette before us. He was just two steps ahead.

'You should be somewhere around here,' he said, and touched my foot with a thin metal walking stick. When his stick touched me, he stopped. He didn't seem to be looking at us but up in the sky.

'Now I've got you,' he said. 'I couldn't have recognised you if you hadn't described your clothes in detail! Now, tell me how you could get lost in this no-man's land.'

We were startled to discover before us an elderly man who was totally blind. I kept silent for a moment, not knowing what to say. Then I said, 'We lost the train. We got down and then must have stepped too far away from it.'

'Like children who stray too far from home and lose their way back,' said the blind man. 'This is what being blind is like if it happens to you later in life.'

'Sorry, we didn't mean to offend you,' I said.

'I know, don't take it seriously,' the man said. I was only joking. You must have figured out that I am blind from the sound of my walking stick as I came toward you.'

I felt like giving him a nasty answer. 'No, from its colour, from its white tip.'

'Amazing. I took this stick thinking that the other one would not be visible in the fog. Actually, I normally don't use my white-tipped stick. I don't like it when people recognize my blindness. You have good eyes, young man,' he said and continued on: 'Madam, we haven't been introduced yet, but I am happy to meet you.'

I rushed to give an answer: 'Sorry sir, but this is not a lady. My companion is male. I was just joking about the bikini.'

The man frowned and was just about to say something when I interrupted: 'My friend is a deaf mute, he can't answer you.'

'Unfortunately he also cannot answer you. I regret that you make jokes on his account. I know you had no bad intentions but it was disrespectful, young man. So this is the fellow who was calling for help. Nice to meet you, young man,' he said and smiled. 'Never mind. Now let me offer you both a cup of tea. Tell your friend to follow me too.'

'Thank you,' I said, 'but the train may leave any minute.'

The man turned in the direction he came from and shouted: 'Engineer, how much longer do you need?'

'It will take at least a half hour,' shouted someone from far away.

'Did you hear that? Come on, let's go. Our café makes wonderful tea and it's open all night,' he said.

'Why didn't they answer us from the train when we were shouting?' I asked. 'Didn't anybody hear us? We screamed so much, asking for help.'

'They did answer. I came to help you,' said the man.

My companion had not understood what was going on but could not take his eyes off the old man. He was very impressed by his blindness. He scrutinized the man's face, his stick, his feet, his hands. I touched his arm to make him look at me and repeated aloud and expressively so he could read my lips: 'This gentleman is inviting us for a cup of tea.'

He couldn't comprehend. One couldn't expect him to. These words were so strange given the situation we were in. Repeating my words I pretended to hold a cup of tea and stir in the sugar. This time he understood but his eyes were full of questions. I nodded my head positively and he gave me an approving sound.

The blind man said, 'Fine then, let's go. The café is not far.'

I hesitated. 'Fine, but how are we going to find our way back to the train?' I asked.

'Don't make things so complicated,' said the man impatiently. 'I am going to bring you back. Give me your hand. Also hold you friend's hand. Don't let go! I don't want you to break your necks in this fog. If you fall and hit your head there is nothing I can do. You know I have to hear your voice to find you. Also don't rely on the dogs. They can't find you either in this fog. Their noses don't function when their eyes can't see. Anyway, in this town you can't find a dog to track anyone. Come on now, forward march!'

We took a couple of steps holding hands but could not walk easily. I felt as though I would bump into something at each step and my friend seemed to feel the same. Our blind guide said, 'Follow my steps at the same stride and pace. Imagine me to be the head of a folk dancing group, not a blind guide. Try to fit your body rhythms to mine.'

In an effort to relate these instructions to my friend, still holding his hand I gently raised our arms up and down like flying movements in the fog. He understood and tried to fall in step. Again, his little joyful screams were heard. Our blind guide started laughing. 'These deaf mutes are always joyful, even when following a blind man!'

After a couple of moments we began to march in harmony. The man was walking unexpectedly fast.

'We are walking on a flat surface,' he said. 'This will continue until we reach the café. Here is a broad square. There are no salient parts that could make us fall, nor is there anybody to bump into. Nobody but me would wander about in this fog. We get fog here frequently. I enjoy myself when the fog comes, and when it disappears everybody rejoices except me. Now tell me, which is better, clear or fog? Hard to decide, isn't it?'

I felt I had to say something. 'But seeing people are the majority. Fog is no good for them,' I said.

'It is wrong to think that what the majority wants is good. In such foggy weather, I show them the way, bring the sick to the hospital or the doctor to the sick.'

'Are you the only blind man around?' I asked.

'Yes, unfortunately,' said the old man. 'This place is smaller than you think. There were two other blind men here but they left a couple of years ago to work in a big city. I heard that their workplace was very well lit. Isn't that funny?'

A couple of steps further on, the ground seemed to slant slightly upward.

'Are we climbing a hill?' I asked.

'No, we are almost there,' he said. 'On our right is a 200-year-old fountain... Now we are right in front of it. You should be able to see the reliefs on it. 28 steps further and we will be at the café.'

And, truly 28 steps later we were standing at a doorstep. The old man found the door with his stick, tried to push it back, but it was closed. 'Do you see any lights at the window?'

'No,' I said.

'Look at that. They are closed again. Sometimes when it is foggy they close the café.'

'Why shouldn't they?' I said. 'You said yourself that

people don't wander around in the fog. What's the use of a café without customers?'

'This café is open 24 hours a day. Two brothers run the place. One of them works in the day, the other at night. They change shifts every month. Wouldn't it be better if one would always work by night and the other by day? I couldn't quite figure out which wears them out more, working by day or working by night. Anyway that's their business, but it makes me sorry as this is no way to run a café that is open all night. Such a café is a security, like a hospital emergency service. It is important for you to know that it's always open. Maybe you go there at midnight just once in forty years but it should always be kept open.'

'I agree with you now,' I said to the man.

'I wore you out for nothing,' he said. 'Actually I could have taken you to my place, but it's a little bit far. If you came some other time at an earlier hour, I would be very glad to host you in my home, I assure you.'

'Thank you for the invitation,' I said. 'I would also like to see you again, but let us get back to our train now.'

'Fine,' he said, 'but also tell your friend what's going on so that he may know we are heading back to the train.'

'You're right, excuse me,' I said.

'Apologise to him, not to me.'

I turned to my deaf friend and said, 'We are going back to the train.' He nodded.

'Sorry for sending you back without offering you anything,' said our guide as he stretched out his hand to me. We all held hands again and walked in the direction we came from. Everyone was silent for a while, each seemingly lost in our own thoughts. I sensed for an instant that my blind guide had pressed my hand.

'What's going on?' I whispered.

He gave no answer, turned right, stopped a little, stopped again. Then he took a deep breath. 'Honeysuckle,' he said, 'how nice they smell.'

I also noticed a distinct smell of honeysuckle. Our guide took one more deep breath. 'I haven't smelled such a pure white honeysuckle for a long time,' he said. As if sensing the question that passed through my mind, he continued talking while stepping ahead, 'The fact that I cannot see colours doesn't mean that I cannot call them by name,' he said.

After a couple of steps, a huge silhouette appeared before us.

'Here we are,' I said, 'the train is in view.'

'Still five or six steps to go,' our guide said and stopped after three steps.

My deaf mute friend let go of my hand and grabbed onto the steps of the train. Clearly now he felt himself safe again. Still holding our guide's hand I said, 'Thank you so much. This was an outing I will never forget. It was incredible. I would like to come and see you again.'

'I would be glad to see you too, young fellow. You can also bring along your friend here, or others. You can invite anybody who would like to chat with a blind man in the fog. I owe you a cup of tea anyway, don't you forget.'

He appeared to sense where my friend was, and shouting in his direction he said, 'Good-bye to you, too. I would like to get to know you better,' and waved.

He turned to me and said, 'Please give my best wishes to your friend and say good-bye.'

Then he turned about abruptly. First his vision, then the sound of his stick and his footsteps melted into the fog.

We climbed onto the train, shut the car door and headed for our compartment. My friend entered and threw himself on his seat. Soon the train began to move. My friend was gazing out the window. After a couple of minutes we noticed the fog had dispersed and houses and lights had become visible. My friend took out a paper and pen from his bag, put the bag on his knees, wrote something on the paper and handed it to me.

He wrote: 'What a fog that was! The man was quite

interesting. I was very excited while we were walking, but the thing that really got to me was the delicious smell of the honeysuckle. I have never smelled such a white scent. It was like silk. Could you write down what you talked about with the old man?'

I nodded and wrote underneath: 'How many empty pages have you got?'

Translated from the Turkish by Carol Stevens Yürür

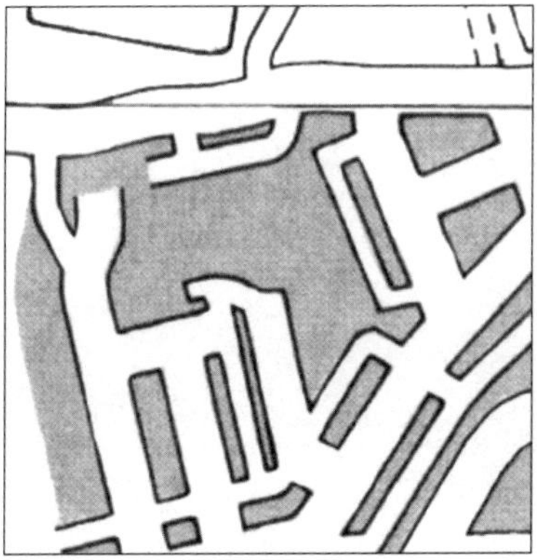

Calcutta

INGO SCHULZE

for Günther Grass

This was three weeks ago, on a Tuesday. The forecast had been for rain, but it was clear and sunny all day. After putting in my two hours of practice, I ate an early lunch and set to work mowing the lawn. The plan was gardening for this week, the garage and the snow tyres the week after – dealing with the car just in general – then came cleaning out the gutters and another go at the garden, and finally, as my last outdoor chore before snow set it, the graves. If you wait until the week before Remembrance Sunday, the cemetery car park is full.

I first noticed her standing at the threshold of her back door and gazing my way. By *her* I mean Becker's wife. We generally refer to our neighbours only in the plural, the Beckers – him, her, and their three kids, Sandra, Nancy, and Kevin.

Becker's wife didn't respond when I called over. I repeated my 'hello, hello' and waved. She kept on looking in my direction, but didn't react. On Sunday, that is two days before, she had brought us the mousetrap and we'd thanked her with a jar of quince jam.

I hadn't the faintest what could have got her ticked off at us over the course of the previous forty-eight hours. I detached the half-full basket from the mower. But instead of emptying it into the blue plastic bag – which would have meant turning my back to her – I carried it to the compost heap behind the garage. I'm always amazed at how fast grass and our little hard apples are transformed into a kind of glop. The stupid thing is we have no real use for it. What we need is mulch to keep the weeds from shooting up over our heads, and good mulch is expensive.

I reattached the basket to the mower. When I straightened up I automatically looked in her direction, gave another wave, shouted, 'The last time!' – I meant mowing the lawn – and attempted a smile. She stood there like a figure in a waxwork museum.

I went back to work and the pace picked up, since there were no apples lying in the grass and only a few drifted leaves.

Maybe I should say something about the mouse, about the mouse and the mosquitoes. Saturday night Martina had woken me up. 'Do you hear that? Don't you hear it?' She sounded just a little hysterical. 'A mouse! Don't you hear it?' The mouse must have scampered in at the window. There had been frost the past few mornings. Martina claimed mice had no trouble clambering up a stucco wall, especially if it was overgrown with a grapevine.

A mousetrap didn't even occur to us, as if that was old-fashioned, obsolete. Martina's plan was to lure the Findeisens' cat over, and I was supposed to move one cabinet after the other away from the wall. There was no mention of a mousetrap until noon, when she was hanging out the washing and told Becker's wife all about it.

The two green interlocking boxes looked more like a homemade telescope. Inside was a triggered pedal, so that when the mouse ran over it the door slammed shut behind. Becker's wife had recommended using sponge cake. Sponge cake was sure to catch any mouse. As I said, that had been two days ago, and I knew of no reason to feel guilty.

And then I just couldn't take it anymore. I left the

mower standing in the middle of the lawn and walked over to her.

'I bought a sponge cake,' I said. 'Would you like a piece?' I wanted to add that even stale sponge cake tasted good with Martina's jam. But she interrupted me.

'Keep your fingers crossed for us,' she repeated more loudly. With every step she took the legs of her black leather trousers rubbed together – a sound somewhere between a squeak and a crunch. 'If you want to do something for us, cross your fingers.'

As she spoke Becker's wife braced herself against the clothes pole and stared at me almost savagely.

Standing between the fence and the quince tree, I listened to her and had no idea how I would ever be able to make my retreat.

Kevin was in a coma. It had happened in front of the theatre, between the two construction sites.

She described it all in great detail. I might even say she got caught up in it, pressing both hands to her ribs and pelvis, slapping her thighs, only to begin squeezing her temples between the heels of both hands and attempting to turn her head, but holding it in place as if caught in a vice. Her jumper had inched up to her navel.

Becker's wife began to weep. I was about to scale the fence and take her hand in mine, when their telephone rang.

She left the back door ajar. So I waited. After a few minutes I pushed the mower over to the fence, dragged the extension cord over, and set to work again in view of her back door, never letting it out of my sight. I assumed Becker's wife was telling somebody what she had just told me, and wondered if she was making the same gestures as she held the phone, but with only one hand touching her body.

Instead of bothering to bend over to empty the mower basket, I went into a squat and, slipping the plastic bag around it, upended it all at once. I worked as if I were under the watchful eye of a supervisor.

To be honest I was relieved that the reason for her strange behaviour wasn't because of some misunderstanding between us – if there has to be a dispute, better one with your colleagues than your neighbours. At home you need your peace and quiet.

Neighbourliness requires nothing more than a greeting and a few extra words. That's no problem in summer. And when there's nothing more to do in the garden, you don't see much of one another, even if your back doors are only forty feet apart.

I rang the doorbell at the Beckers' and the Findeisens' just once all last winter, under the pretext of needing a couple of onions and a lemon. You have to do that sort of thing on weekends of course. And bring back at least twice as much on Monday. You want them to know they can depend on you. Moreover, hardly a week goes by that I don't accept a package for somebody on the block. And I'm willing to do other favours as well, all anybody needs to do is ask.

And so I kept my eye on her back door, but somehow missed the moment when she closed it. Had Becker's wife noticed that I had long since finished with mowing around the quince tree? Had I looked ridiculous?

It was on the little strip of grass between the street and the house that I found the schnapps bottles. There was always at least one, but this time there were three: two bottles of Golden Meadow and one of Little Coward. A fourth one missing its label had been set upside down on the narrow brick border around our herb bed. Evidently homeless people had taken a break at our place on their way to the shelter. That also explained the dog shit, which luckily the mower cleared as it passed over.

I always assumed we had come to some tacit agreement with the homeless people: they were to screw the tops back on the bottles and not fling them into the street or against the wall of the house. Most of the time I just tossed these wino bottles into the rubbish, although normally we carefully separate metal caps from glass. But tossing four of them into the container at once – no, I couldn't do it. On the other hand, the idea of screwing off the caps disgusted me – those belong in the yellow bag – plus having to rinse out the bottles before putting them in the container for throwaway glass. I propped all four against the dustbin. Maybe Martina would come up with a solution.

That particular afternoon the grass smelled at times like sorrel, then like fish, and then again like it had in the spring. It even left a taste like sliced cucumbers in my mouth.

Around five o'clock Becker himself came home and vanished into the house. He works in a computer shop. At one time he had been part of the cadre responsible for selling Planeta printing presses worldwide. Martina always holds up his example to me – he had just rolled his sleeves up. Because he, or so she claimed, didn't think he was too good for any job.

He's one of those people who can eat whatever they want and never get fat – and pride themselves on the fact. He almost always wears faded blue jeans, with a big bunch of keys hanging from one belt loop to announce his comings and goings like a cowbell.

Ten minutes later the Beckers drive off with the two girls.

Although it was almost dark and I had done more than enough for one day, I went on working. I prefer to go back into the house along with Martina, or after her on those rare occasions when she makes supper. Nowadays she's frequently late, a whole hour on that particular Tuesday. I waited until she was sitting in the kitchen to tell her the news.

I had taken note of every detail – from the broken cheekbones, collarbones, and ribs, to the pelvis and legs, down to the decrease in cerebral pressure, and how Nancy, who had witnessed the whole thing, was getting psychological counselling.

Holding her head between her hands, Martina looked as

if she were covering her ears. She often sits there like that when she's tired. I think we were both relieved to find Felix at the door.

In May he had joined a group of fellow students in a shared flat not far from Market Square, a real tumbledown dump. He's been paying the fifty marks rent himself. I don't know where he is getting the money from.

Martina told him about the Beckers. I was hoping she would forget some detail so I could chime in. She asked me how the driver was doing. I shrugged.

'Close call,' was all that Felix managed to come up with in reply to Martina's report. She wanted to know what he meant by that. Felix had his mouth full and chopped at the air with the edge of his hand. 'The crash happened practically next door to us, close call.'

I waited for Martina to say something. But nothing apt came to her either.

Ever since he moved out Felix and I have been getting along better again. We both think Martina's new hair-do is silly. From a distance it looks like she's wearing a beret.

Felix was still eating when Martina stood up with a start. She ran upstairs ahead of us. 'Nothing this time either,' she said, eyeing me.

It was only then I realised how much I hated having a mousetrap in the house. I'm even certain that at that moment the feeling crept over me that those interlocked metal boxes were like bad luck magnets. We placed the trap closer to the window and crumbled more sponge cake.

It stayed sunny all week. I practiced every day from nine to eleven. I think my playing is pretty good, even if of late there is nobody to hear me. My bow technique especially has improved quite a bit. Bow technique and etudes. I had never really had the time before. Bach and Mozart as my reward. Afterwards I concentrate on housework.

When I'm not in the mood for practicing, I listen to music. All I ever ask for are CDs. The public library doesn't have many to lend out. Of late I've been listening to our records again. What a feeling to lift the tone arm to the edge and slowly shift the lever and watch the stylus make contact! The complete Beethoven with Masur, Schumann with Sawallisch. I've listened to them since I was fifteen, sixteen. I could conduct them. I could direct it all by heart. I've always worked as a construction engineer, usually as project manager. But deep down I'm a musician.

Becker's wife had taken sick leave. I watched her open the door for her kids. Her front door doesn't open onto the street, but is at the side, directly opposite our bathroom window.

As soon as her husband came home, they would drive off, with Sandra and Nancy usually with them. They'd come back after two or three hours.

That Friday Becker's wife was just returning from shopping when I went to check the post. She had lost weight. She looked good. I nodded to her, but then turned back as if I had the wrong key.

'We're keeping our fingers crossed,' was the statement I had prepared for any eventuality. She would hardly have been interested in news about the mouse. Not that there was any, although the first thing Martina did when she got home from work was to run upstairs. 'Nothing this time either,' she'd say.

I added a piece of ham to the sponge cake. Normally our eyes take only a few days to integrate a strange object into a larger familiar image. But I found the thing more and more disgusting – the very idea of having to hold both boxes in my hands with a mouse running back and forth inside. Or would it play dead? Once we got to that point I wanted to call the Becker kids over. It would add some variety to their lives. And they could take the trap with them.

It was always Martina who heard the mouse. I wouldn't even have noticed a mouse without her. What plagued me at night were the mosquitoes. I always thought mosquitoes die in the autumn. This year it looked as if they were going to spend the winter with us. At first I thought they were biting just me – one even managed to creep up inside a nostril. But come morning I saw that Martina had more bites than me – so I had no reason to complain.

Last year around the same time when I was tidying up the attic, I discovered that a whole army of spiders had marched through the skylight. But mosquitoes in November is an entirely different matter, wouldn't you say?

That last week in October I had also taken care of the gutters and had cut back the grapevine. Of course I also take care of the chores – from shopping to cleaning the house. I like doing it.

If Martina were the one to stay at home, the world would find that perfectly normal. Men, however, are always telling me how much they have to do. And if I say that I'm up to my ears in work too, they grin and give me a dumb look.

You automatically take a back seat of course. I never sit up watching television longer than Martina. When she gets up in the morning I head for the kitchen to make breakfast. As long as Felix was still living here, it was me who woke him up and chased him out of bed.

I think Martina likes having hardly any housework to do and always having somebody who's there to greet her, who's set the table for her. Everything has its good side. And as long as the money covers expenses... It used to be perfectly normal for somebody to stay at home full time.

The thing is, once Lippendorf was finished, I put in an application with every department, even PR work. Who should know a project better than somebody who helped build it? After all, I knew that box inside and out. Do you suppose they gave me a chance? They didn't even call me in for an interview. It's all a matter of cliques, whether old or new. You either side with one bunch or the other. Otherwise you're just out of luck. The unemployment office had the bright idea of sending me to a free newspaper. I was supposed to polish doorknobs looking for advertisers. 'I built a power plant,' I said and was out the door. If I ever take on something like that, it's all over, I'm washed up. I don't need to explain that, do I?

Early in the second week with the mouse, I had just come in from the garden and was about to take a shower when I heard our car in the driveway, and seconds later Martina's footsteps. Just as you can automatically hum the rest of a familiar melody, I waited for the sound of her key in the front door. I stepped into the tub, but then turned the water off again when nothing more happened. I interrupted my shower a couple times to call Martina's name. Finally, my hair still wet, I walked out into the garden. Martina and Becker's wife were standing at the fence. Martina had done some grocery shopping. So I had the excuse of offering to take both bags into the house. I unpacked it all, made some tea, set the table, and thumbed through the newspaper inserts.

'Makes a person feel truly sorry for them,' Martina said after having drunk a glass of apple juice. I was annoyed that she took it for granted that I had once again put together a nice meal and then had to wait for her.

From then on they stood there every evening. Becker's wife would even come outside in the dark just so she could talk with Martina.

So we were kept well-posted. Martina talked about how much Andrea, Becker's wife, missed her Kevin every time she turned around. 'An adult,' Martina said, 'would no longer be alive. But with children there's still hope even when doctors are at the end of their tether.'

I thought about how even in cases like this a certain kind of routine sets in. You drive to the hospital, hold your child's hand for a few hours, convince yourself he's just sleeping, talk with the doctors, have them explain what they'll be trying to accomplish with the next operation, and cry a little before you leave. The garage door signals that they're back home. Evidently you have to give it a kick to open or close it. One after the other three motion-sensitive lights go on, and the four Beckers march into the house Indian file as if moving across a stage.

Until yesterday at any rate there was nothing new in the mouse department. I was constantly greeted with Martina's message of 'Nothing this time either.' I was told I ought to pull the furniture out from the wall a little more at least. The back of one cabinet had been nibbled at. 'You see!' Martina exclaimed. 'Just look at that!'

How was the mouse my fault? Can you tell me that?

I went out into the garden and set to work weeding. The best time for pulling weeds from between the walkway cracks is when everything is damp and nothing is growing anymore.

Suddenly somebody said, 'You've just about got it licked,' or something like that. Even though he was wearing his bunch of keys as always, I hadn't noticed the head of the Becker household.

Becker was resting his hands on the fence, and it was obvious this was going to be awkward and I couldn't just keep on squatting there.

'Well?' I said, 'How's it going?'

'You ever been to Calcutta?'

I thought maybe he had misspoken and meant the Indian restaurant that had just opened up on the grounds of the old Russian barracks. Luckily I just said, 'No.'

'That's a city you've got to see,' he exclaimed. 'You don't understand one thing about this world if you haven't experienced Calcutta.'

He started in and there seemed to be no end to his tale. The whole thing sounded a little odd to me, but I listened all the same. At first I was still thinking about Martina – about me and Martina – but then I just listened to what the head of the Becker household had to say.

'You planning to go back?' I asked when he paused to blow his nose.

'Wait just a sec,' he said, turned around, and went back into the house. He returned with a heavy necklace, corals alternating with silver balls.

'Here, have a look. Stuff like this goes for a song there.'

I raised my dirty hands. He misunderstood and hung the necklace over my right forearm.

It was really heavy. I examined it while he went on talking. After ten minutes he took the necklace back and wrapped it around his wrist. It was already dark when he stuck out his hand to say goodbye.

I rang my mother that same evening. Sometime I'd like to actually ask her why she hadn't let me enrol in the high school that specialises in music. Have you ever heard of a musician getting fired? I haven't.

Lately my mother always wants to know if I'm sleeping okay. That's become her criterion for general well-being. I told her I'd be sleeping well enough if weren't for damned mosquitoes.

'That's funny,' she exclaimed, 'I've got bites every morning, real mosquito bites.' Now that was eerie, I thought, right out of Hitchcock. If those little beasts were suddenly going crazy at the end of the millennium, that meant something. On the other hand that might get things moving, there might be a lot of new jobs, cram courses for trained exterminators.

Last night I left the window wide open – that way it wouldn't be so cosy for mosquitoes.

I assume it was the Beckers' garage door that woke me up. I heard their car start and back out onto the driveway. I recognized Becker's voice. He was talking to his wife. Then the girls came trotting out. He told them both to go back to bed. All I heard from her was a kind of a clucking and that sound her leather pants makes when she walks. Both car doors slammed shut almost simultaneously. I didn't get up. The girls stayed outside for a while. I could only make out individual words.

I was surprised that they left the garage door open. Maybe they thought they'd be back soon. It was a foolish thing to do though – an open garage with bikes, tyres, and all sorts of tools.

Further off in town I could hear a few cars and a freight train approaching. We've lived here long enough to recognize all the sounds. But they travel this well only on November nights.

Gradually I could make out the stems of the leafless grape vines framing the window. They looked like the feelers of giant snails or like V's for victory, or like the feet of animals you might assemble out of matchsticks. As it grew lighter and the Findeisens' car drove off, the stems seemed to turn reddish. Where they thicken at the end they look like cotton buds. For a moment I thought I smelled alcohol, and thought of the homeless people and their bottles. I had no idea what Martina had done with those.

She slept until the alarm went off, threw me a quick glance, and sat up on the edge of the bed. Before getting up, she stretched her arms over her head. I used to pull her back into bed sometimes.

I could sense that it wouldn't even take her asking me a question—just one single word, something totally trivial – and I'd lose it. I've slowly learned to live with the feeling. It hardly scares me anymore. It comes over me with almost soothing regularity. And I give in to it – but of course only when I'm alone. Other people, especially those who think they know me, would find it upsetting. Basically it's nothing more than bleeding radiators. It has to be done every now and then.

Of course it was clear to me that I had to get up. The timing was tight, and if nothing had been done when Martina emerged from the bathroom, she'd have to leave without breakfast. Pulling the car out and sitting there waiting at the front gate wouldn't help either.

I thought I heard the Beckers' car. I raised my head from

the pillow and listened. From that position I could see the mousetrap. It was still wide open.

And then I heard the bathroom door and Martina going downstairs. Step by step, stair by stair, finally her heels striking the kitchen tiles and the squeak – or more like the whinny – of the fridge door.

Suddenly it was clear to me that the mouse – presuming it was still alive – had been listening to these same sounds and noises, although maybe somewhat muted by the cabinet. And that it could probably tell whether somebody was going up or down the stairs, and that it felt frightened when steps approached, and maybe even joy or at least relief when they moved away again, though that didn't change its situation. And I understood that all I needed to do was close the trap, carry it out into the garden, and come evening tell Martina that the mouse had shot away like an arrow. I was sorry I hadn't thought of that earlier, and how this was a great a moment to give the trap back, to be rid of it at last – right now, when I could hear the Beckers laughing. I only had to go to the window, and I'd see the Beckers, all five of them, coming up the hill and waving at us over and over. Although they were still a good distance off, I spotted the huge sponge cake they were carrying, a gift for their hosts. I still remember wanting to compare their three kids, scampering ahead in their bright outfits, with butterflies in a flowery meadow. 'Like butterflies, like butterflies,' I wanted to call out to them.

I can still recall the kids, them and how the sound of their footsteps came closer and closer. Have you ever actually been to Calcutta?

Translated from the German by John E. Woods

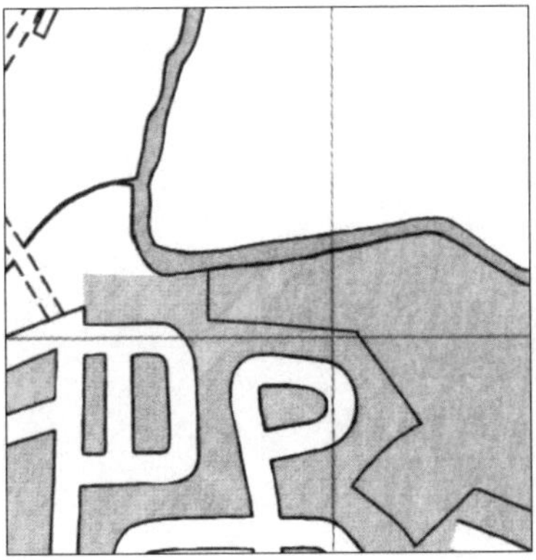

The Closeted Pensioner

Micheál Ó Conghaile

I'm living this long while now in the toilet. Well settled in. I've locked myself in. And I've never been happier in my life. My adventurous days pass quickly. I'm not exactly sure – and couldn't care less – how long I'm here. Years maybe. What difference does it make. Time doesn't count here. No clock on the wall in front of me. Or alarm. Or angelus. No deadlines. No calendar, moon or tide. The only date I remember is the day I finished with the civil service – that fateful day on which I took early retirement: and straight into the jacks with purposeful stride. Just like that. The same evening! Now that was something. And I'm thriving ever since.

    Sure, they tried to stop me. Head me off at the creek. Over and over again they pleaded with me to reconsider. They put me under a lot of pressure. A lot of warnings. The little woman had the biggest problem with it and soon the whole family were behind her. 'You're a thundering disgrace!' 'What will the neighbours say.' 'Have you no sense at all.' 'You can't stay there you know.' What a chorus. 'And why can't I?' says I. 'Who's to stop me?' I was getting bull-headed. 'It's my life and I can do what I want with it. Get a life,' I told them, 'every blasted boring one of you. Anyways, don't ye go into the upstairs loo yerselves!' That got them. They went ape-shit altogether. They started kicking at the door like a child locked in his room after being beaten for no reason.

'Going to the toilet is not the same as taking up residence there,' suggested the missus, 'everybody goes to the toilet once in a while and it's an acceptable fact of nature.'

'I don't, do I?' says myself. 'You're wrong again woman, as usual. Isn't that one of the reasons I'm here. I'm here because I'm here, because I decided to go on early pension and come in here. I won't have to go to the loo again for the rest of my life. Let ye be off now and mark my words, ye pack of divils!'

I believe this sermon sobered them up a bit. They knew well I was right. They left me for a while. I suppose they thought surely I'd get fed up in time and come crawling out. But I'm not in the least put out here and there's no danger of that either. That's where they were wrong from the beginning. They thought I'd emerge in the middle of the night or early morning at latest, my tail between my legs. No tail I'm telling you. I much prefer this place to the outside world, I'm as oblivious as my arse... except when they start annoying me out there.

Of course, I'm not actually sitting on the toilet all of the time. Only some of the time really. I keep myself busy. I'd go crazy otherwise. I've the walls covered in graffiti. Tiredness of the wrist is all that stops me from writing. I listen to the flush every time I pull the chain. I know how many drops it takes to fill the cistern. Much puffing and snorting dispels odours. And thinking – I do a lot of thinking, thinking about women I fell in love with, conversations and arguments I had, going out visiting at night, days in the office... there's no limit to me at all and the thoughts crowding my head. And dreaming as well – my imagination taking flight, from birth to death, transmigration, the whole shebang. My head is always bursting at the seams with the strangest dreams of every variety. I've them all well listed by now – stored away and graded under each subject category. There's more of them than would fit in the most powerful computer. New dreams are filed away each morning, when I awake and make a comparative study of them. But there's more than dreams to keep me occupied. I sing songs and recite reams of poetry, dredging them from the recesses of my mind, blowing the dust off them. I say my prayers, of course, a few times a day like a good Christian and say the rosary every night, counting the Aves on my fingers and thumbs. I myself respond to the prayers, naturally enough, and sometimes you'd think there's more than one of me in the toilet. I pray most fervently and most piously and the orisons rebound from the companionable walls.

Other times, as a brain-limbering exercise, I'd ask myself a riddle and try to figure out the answer... which is the longest, the goose's beak or the gander's? Which cow yields most milk? What goes up but doesn't come down? Which is closest to you – yesterday or tomorrow? Working out riddles is great sport entirely. I make up a number of new riddles for myself as well, in order to create answers which turn out to be right. And who can contradict me? I don't suppose anyone else makes up the same riddles, not to mention the answers. I drive the wife round the bend when I shout one of my riddles. They nearly always get it wrong outside and even if they get it right the odd time, I tell them they're greatly mistaken and make up a new answer on the spot. Sure, they wouldn't know the difference, the poor misfortunates. And that's how it goes.

When I need a rest from the riddles, I try out some other trick – I've no want of pastimes. The family tree – I've worked out who my great-grandfather was on my mother's side long ago... I count all the cousins. Classify distant relations. Working out who exactly is related to whom around here. Those who were engaged once and never married. Those who don't talk to each other and why they might have it in for each other. Those who don't talk to each other though their families do. Those who usedn't talk to each other though their families did. Those who usedn't talk to each other but do now – or those who were the best of buddies and wouldn't look at each other today, crossing to the other side of the read of necessary. And necessary it is...

Now, how could I be fed up with life and all that'd be going on. And that's nothing. Whatever the way it is when I start on the physical work, time flies in the toilet. It's essential I keep myself fit and supple at all times. And I do, faith. A couple of hundred press-ups daily – sit-ups, heel-ups and whatever's up with yourself. I'd do an hour of stationary jogging a day. The equivalent of a good few road miles and it's better at it I'm getting. Getting faster all the time. If I'd a stopwatch I could judge the progress I'm making, but I haven't... A pity I haven't one of those bikes that are stuck to the floor. I could stick it to the ceiling and be pedalling away for myself. Not to worry, I'm as fit as a fiddle the way I am, and as sound as a salmon. I'm much better off here. Now! And they thought I could do nothing inside here, apart from the obvious. But I can have a full, creative life here in the toilet. Anyone thinking of going out on pension should think of the toilet, I tell them. I'd be dead and buried long ago if I were anywhere else. I haven't aged a bit in here – au contraire – which can't be said about the others... They're sprawled on the couch, enthralled by satellite television. If I were one of them sure I'd only be a slave. A zombie.

'Wouldn't you think of going to Spain?' says she under the door.

'I could think of it,' says I. I gave her some rope, knowing she'd hang herself soon.

'It would do you good. A lot of pensioners go to Spain. They like the heat. I wouldn't mind it one bit myself.'

'I know they go,' says I, 'especially if they have the arthritis. I never stopped a pensioner going to Spain, did I?'

'You didn't, dear.'

'Well, let no one stop this pensioner in here so,' says I.

That was the end of Spain. A bloodless victory, I'd say.

THE CLOSETED PENSIONER

It wasn't quite as easy to rout the parish priest when she brought him to hear my confession and to prepare my soul, as she said, seeing I hadn't been to confession in ages.

'Divil a confession,' says I. 'Pull the other one. What sort of sinning could I do here. Did I steal something or covet the neighbour's wife. Did I kill someone in here. Did I tell an injurious lie. Did I drag God's name through the mire for no reason. Did I give bad example. Was I gambling in here or driving at a hundred miles per hour. Or any of the other thousand extra sins in the revised Catechism. Huh! Half of them weren't even invented when I came in here. How could I commit sins that weren't there? Do ye know anything? Sure the toilet isn't an occasion of sin. This place is free of the devil's wiles and temptations.'

'Fine! Fine!' It was the priest who spoke, trying his best to placate me. 'We're for your own good. We know the regard you have for the place you find yourself in.' He began to brown-nose me then and called me a gentleman. 'We're all sinners, each and every one of us. But if you like, sir, you can make your confession from where you are. You don't even have to come out. You can bend a knee there inside the door and I'll be able to absolve you through the keyhole. In that way you can cleanse your soul and stay where you are. It's your soul I'm trying to save.'

'Cleanse my soul,' I shouted, 'through this measly keyhole. My soul is it? Piss off now or it's my hole you'll be hearing from, a forceful fart from my hole, through the keyhole and into your earhole. Feck off with you!'

'Now, now patience my son. No need to be rude. Your lady wife and myself are only thinking of your welfare. You're there now years. It is not good for man to be alone.'

'Don't be stupid,' says I. 'Aren't Elvis and Rushdie in here keeping me company lots of the time. We play cards too. You bet. Big time.'

'Now, now,' said the priest, 'it's not any younger you're getting but – alas – older, like the rest of us... You know what

I'm saying. You could... you could... God between us and all harm... you could kick the bucket any day now.'

I laughed out loud. I laughed and laughed. 'Bucket-schmucket! It chokes you to say it, doesn't it. I could DIE, DIE, D-I-E,' I screamed, luxuriating in the word and in its echo all round me, before collapsing in another paroxysm of laughter.

'Holy Father,' says I, standing on my head at this stage with stitches of laughter and speaking through the crack in the door, 'Father,' says I, 'I'll tell you something seeing as you don't know... Do you hear me?' I took two sharp breaths. 'People don't die in the toilet. Do you understand? Oh, they die in the bedroom, the sitting room, the dining room, the kitchen, out on the street or in the garden, sometimes on the stairs if they fall down and even in the bathroom. Yes, the bathroom – if they slip coming out of the bath or drown in the tub or – God look down on us – if they cut their wrists – but not in the jacks... Not in the jacks! People don't snuff it in the jacks, end of story. Right?'

I was breathless after my monologue. I drew my breath again as quickly as I could, so that I could launch into the rest of my eloquent speech.

'People do not die in the toilet,' I reiterated. 'May God give you sense, Father, and may His blessed Son take pity on your empty head, but did you ever hear it tell, "Mr. X. died today... at home, in the jacks." Did you ever hear that? You never did. Never, and do you want to know why? Because it doesn't happen, see? Not even in America or in the English newspapers. And anyway, even if it could happen – or was about to happen – it wouldn't be allowed to happen, because they wouldn't let a person snuff it in the loo. People would think it was a disgrace or a scandal or... impolite. And people don't want to be impolite, do they! He'd be taken out of the toilet before he breathed his last, so that they wouldn't have to admit that it was in the loo he died... Anyways, they wouldn't announce his death before they got him into the bed. Father, dear, who'd admit a relation of his died in the toilet? Who...? The smart-alicks of the town, some TV smartypants, asking was he standing up or sitting down when death struck, was it No. 1 or No. 2, Father – we'll say nothing about No. 3. Oh no!'

The poor priest never came back and my soul is still unshriven. I don't think he was much taken by my brand of wisdom. He didn't say so as such but that's my conclusion. I suppose he's busy now sucking a confession out of some old wretch before he croaks it and before what he thinks is a spirit within him soars free. My spirit – if such a thing I harbour – is perfectly OK thank you; and if it's not it won't be the confessor that will make it whole or wheedle me out of here. They all have a plan to get me out. People have so many plans, all of them. Even my lawyer, he's full of plans, nice ones though, but my poor old lawyer won't get me out either. He was outside the other day, the other day... the other something anyway. He knocked on the door – something the others haven't the manners to do – a sprightly little knock as he whistled gaily.

'Excuse me,' says he, interrupting me in the middle of the rosary, 'I wonder could I bother you a moment!'

'You're bothering me as it is,' I replied, 'so it's a bit late for excuses or wondering could you bother me further. Who the hell are you anyway?' – pretending I didn't recognise his voice.

'Your lawyer, of course, who else? Don't say you don't recognise me. Wouldn't you be inside a little cell for life long ago, in the security wing, if it weren't for all the court cases I won on your behalf – I wouldn't mind but you were guilty of each crime and other crimes that never came to light.'

'True for you,' says I in a hushed whisper, 'but don't forget you did well out of it yourself, a few backhands which we needn't mention now... and what about that scam? Never mind. I thought I'd seen the last of you, but you're a good man. What do you want?'

'A signature, what else.'

'What else. How foolish of me. What else would a lawyer want but a signature. What do I have to sign this time?'

'Your will, what else?'

'Not a good sign. But at least I've a will and where there's a will there's a way. You're a much squarer bloke than that rogue priest who was here a while ago wanting me to sign my soul and, sure, whatever soul I had I left it outside when I came in here.'

'I'm glad you're willing to sign it,' says he. 'What'll you leave the wife? I'll take a note of it here.'

'A single bed. Heaven closed to her and Hell as her reward,' says I. That much I knew for sure.

'I'd leave her more if I had it but I haven't. Let her be grateful for that much itself. Everything else is gone.'

'She'll profit rightly by you it seems,' says the lawyer, 'only maybe you're giving her too much.'

'No way. I was never one to give her too much.'

'Now if you would sign these documents.'

'Shove 'em under the door.'

He did.

'But you'll need a witness.'

'Aren't you a witness?'

'But I can't see you.'

'Close one eye and look through the keyhole.'

'OK, it will have to do, I suppose.'

'It will.'

'Well then, everything is settled except for the matter of... where do you wish to be buried?'

'Buried! In the name of God, I'm not going to be buried, unless they bury me alive. I'm as buried as I'll ever be here.'

'Everyone gets buried.'

'They do if they die, but people don't die in the toilet. What do you think I'm doing here only keeping myself alive.

To die in here would be too traumatic for a living person and too dramatic for his people!'

'It would to be sure. You're perfectly right there. But, what would you like us to do with you?'

'Well, nothing really... just leave me be... but, of course, should you wish – later on – or should it become necessary, ye can cremate me. Alive, of course.'

'Cremate you alive! But that's totally –'

'No it's not. C.U. Burn Crematorium. I've come to a special arrangement...'

'Alright! Alright! Very nice, it can be arranged for a reasonable sum, I suppose, but then what do we do with your ashes? Oh, of course, they could be scattered to the winds or exhibited somewhere. It wouldn't be necessary to bury them, but some arrangement would have to be in place.'

'Sure, there wouldn't be a whole lot of me. Keep a pinch for yourself and store it in the egg-timer. You can use it every morning and watch me trickling down.'

'Lovely! Thanks very much and may you have a long life. You'll be very useful to me in the egg-timer – but the rest of the ashes... not too nice to leave them standing around. Your wife, you know, the family, or the greedy rogue priest. You wouldn't want them sinking their claws into you – or your ashes!'

'Not to worry. There's an easy way out of this,' I said. 'I'll be able to plan it all myself. All you have to do is stuff what's left into a condom, when it's cooled of course, and bring it back here to me. Slide it carefully under the door. Be sure it doesn't burst. OK?'

'OK. OK.'

'I can flush it down the toilet whenever I... *should* I choose to do so.'

Translated from the Irish by Gabriel Rosenstock

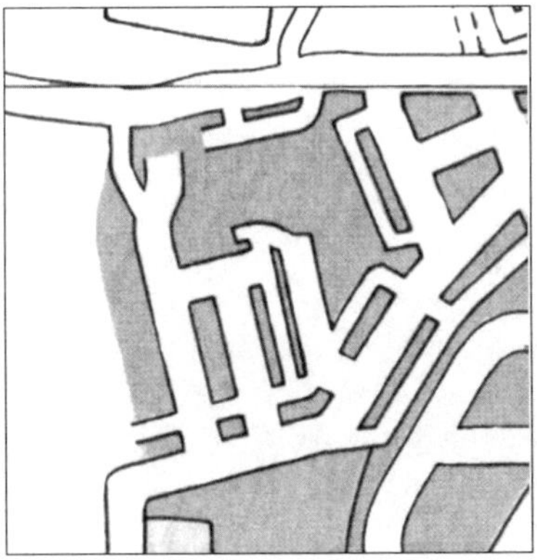

The Water People

Gyrðir Elíasson

In the house next to the sea, lights are burning in the attic, but the lower floor is darkened, and there are a few lights in other houses, these few and small houses, oppressed by the darkness. The house is purple, and attracted a lot of attention in the village at the time, when the sisters painted it themselves, wearing blue overalls. Now everyone has stopped looking at it, as the colour has faded. And the sisters have aged, and their father who stayed with them has long since died and they sometimes feel that they are alone in the world, in this little fjord, even though there are people in the houses around them. This fjord is their world; here eyes were opened and here they will close, when the time comes.

That evening, the older sister sits in a rocking chair on the upper floor and smokes a pipe, watching television. The other sister lies on her bed in the bedroom, the door open into the hall. She is reading an old book, it is Steingrímur Thorsteinsson's *Poems* and she wears glasses on her nose. Now and then, she looks up from the book and into the hall, and sees how the sky-blue flicker from the television lights up her sister's grey hair.

'What are you watching, Nanna?' she says.

'Oh, a crime film,' replies the older sister and the grey-blue smoke wraps around the grey head and blends in with the blue flicker.

'Shall I read you something from Thorsteinsson?' asks the other one. 'Oh, not now, Jónína dear, they are about to kill a man here.' The younger sister sighs on her bed in the room and continues to read, mumbling to herself, very softly. Above the bed is a picture of their parents; a young couple in a photographer's studio in the next fjord, and an artificial landscape in the background. On the wall opposite hangs a picture of Þorsteinn Erlingsson, in a small, round frame.

Then Jónína looks up from her book again and says: 'We should have painted the house this summer, sister.'

Her sister answers, without taking her eyes off the screen: 'First you stop painting your face, then you stop painting a house. We will hardly be painting it from now on. I always thought the colour was rather bold, too. You wanted it like this.'

'Have you forgotten that it was you who picked this colour?'

'Shush, they are loading the gun now,' says the older sister. The glow of the pipe has gone out, and she has stopped rocking.

Jónína reads the book for a good while, then looks up again and says: 'Remember, sister, when we were small and we went up into the Hat Mountain here, and dad went looking for us and found us by the Raven Cliffs, where we were throwing rocks over the edge. Dad was afraid for us then. Do you remember that?'

'Please dear, I am watching the telly here,' and she re-lights the pipe and the chair starts creaking again.

The younger sister sighs, puts the book down on the nightstand and rises from the bed, looks out of the attic window, out into the autumn darkness, onto the shaded ocean.

'Another autumn,' she thinks. 'How many autumns more? We are not Sisters of Hope.'

Through the gunshots the older sister calls into the room. 'Jónína, won't you please heat some tea for us before bed?' 'And what type of tea do you want?' asks the other one blankly and continues to look out the window.

'Just chamomile now I think, it is getting so late,' says Nanna, and the pipe lets out a snorting sound.

Jónína goes down the stairs, turns on a light on the lower floor, heats water on the stove and comes upstairs, carrying a ceramic pot and two mugs.

'Tea for two,' Nanna says cheerfully.

'Yes, if it only were for *two*,' Jónína thinks and puts down the tray with the pot and the mugs. She sits down in a chair beside her sister, who rocks and slurps tea and lights the pipe yet again, until the film is finished.

'Now we go to bed, *sister dear*,' Jónína thinks, but aloud she says: 'Yes, it will be a hard day tomorrow.'

'Will it?' the other one says. 'How do you know? Isn't it just an ordinary day? You are not going to paint the house, are you?'

'It will be a hard day,' Jónína says calmly. 'I know it.'

That night, when the house is ablaze and the billowing smoke rolls up into the starless sky, the sisters resemble giant moths or old fairies in their grey nightgowns, fluttering in the slow breeze off the ocean.

The younger sister carries Steingrímur Thorsteinsson's *Poems* under her arm and stares into the sea of flames, but the older one, her grey hair hanging down, keeps her hands in the pockets of her nightgown.

Then they look at each other.

'Didn't you turn off the stove?' asks the older sister.

'Didn't you put out the pipe?' asks the other one in turn.

'I dreamt badly too, straight after I fell asleep,' sighs the older one.

'It's the television, *sister dear*,' says the other one. 'You should have unplugged it.'

The fire creaks and crackles, its purple colour has now turned to black and the blaze is reflected off the nearby houses. People have woken up and are on their way with water buckets and tubs. An old man, limping, drags a green garden hose behind him through the autumn-coloured grass in the night.

'And with dad always so afraid of fire,' says the younger sister and pulls the picture of her parents from her pocket and gives it to her sister.

'Mum was too, I think,' says Nanna and wipes imaginary dust from the picture, examining it by the glow from the burning house.

'But we are not alone in the world, after all,' says Jónína, and points to the water people who are edging closer.

Translated from the Icelandic by Vera Juliusdottir

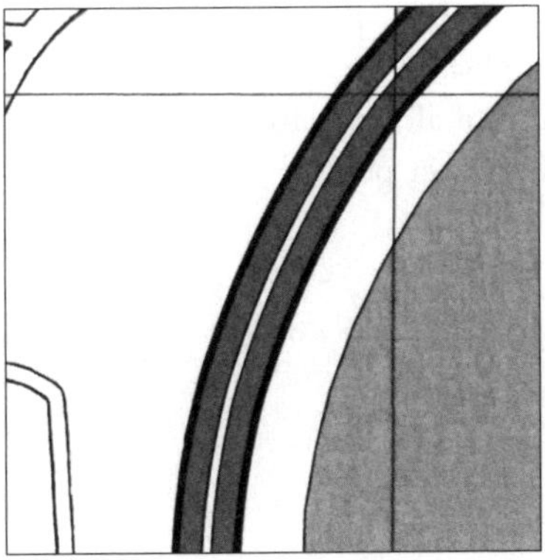

We Did It Because We Had To

Roman Simić

It rained. The road was meandering and wet and he had to drive slowly so that they wouldn't skid, so that they wouldn't slide away.

'Are you cold?' he asked.

She did not reply, she was pretending to be asleep.

He turned the heat up. It was getting dark. There were no houses, no sheep, not a thing by the road. He craved a cigarette. They were on the back seat, in his jacket, with her, he thought for a second or two. 'Pass me the cigarettes.'

She was silent. Without taking his eyes off the road, he felt for the jacket with his hand.

'Don't smoke.'

He looked for her eyes in the rearview mirror. They were closed. 'Why?'

She did not reply.

He watched the chipped white lines emerge and disappear on the road in front of them. 'What?' he asked.

The only thing he heard was the scratching of the wipers on the windscreen.

'We did it because we had to,' he said.

'I just asked you not to smoke.'

He turned on the radio. The car echoed...

'Please...'

'Go f...'

Sharp red lights sparkled before them. The road slowed down. Then became faster.

While they were silent, he thought about them. About the silence, about Vanja. She was always the one talking. He had met her on the street, in front of a phone booth, she had talked so much that he had thought...

'Do you remember...,' but he gave up.

Now, between them, there was the wall, the ice mass, that he felt all over, that lurked from the rearview mirror, in her closed eyes, where he dared not look. He thought they were in a film and that they were driving in a limo, separated by a thick, dark glass which neither of them was able to lower. 'Maybe we should've slept in Zagreb; I could've phoned Joško...'

'Have I told you what I dreamt about last night?' she broke the silence. 'I dreamt that we were at the seaside and that we were collecting sea shells...'

'You've told me.'

'We collected many sea shells, and sea snails, and everything, and everything was great like it...'

He drove slowly now. They were passing through some village. There was no one on the street.

'You said that there was a pearl in one of the shells and we tried to open it, but we couldn't, so you put it in the shallow water so that it would think it was free and that...'

Candles burned in the window frames of the houses by the road. Tricolor flags, all wet with rain, hung down from some of the houses. Some of them were almost touching the ground.

'And when it opened, you slid in a pocket knife, opened it and showed me the pearl, in it, inside, it was the most beautiful thing I had ever seen in my life...'

'Vanja...'

'Then we went down to the beach and met somebody

and he asked us what had happened, and you told him, but when you wanted to show him the pearl, you couldn't find it anymore, it wasn't there, it wasn't in your pocket either, we'd lost it somewhere along the way...'

'What the fuck, stop already!!' He pulled over and turned toward her. 'Haven't I asked you nicely...'

'You have.'

Behind her closed eyes the...

He reached toward her. He couldn't hug her. The seats were in his way. 'My love...'

She sobbed, lay down, and covered her face with her hands. He could not hear anything. He touched her knee, left his hand there.

'Vanja...' He did not know what to say. He looked outside, through the window covered with mist lit by the wet orange light.

'We did it...' Facing tears, he never knew how – he felt stupid. He stopped talking. Finally he covered her with his jacket, took the cigarettes from it and tucked them into his pocket.

'Sleep. I'll wake you up when we get there.' The words sounded hollow, impotent.

He thought he should get out of the car, sit next to her on the back seat and do something.

'Please, drive,' she said.

A passing car honked at them and he realised they were parked at the kerb with their lights off. He turned the engine on. He felt relieved. He moved on. For a moment his hands were shaking on the steering wheel. He tried to think only about the road, to drive carefully, but faster. He managed to do it and he felt calmer. He felt he needed air. He rolled the window down and then rolled it up again. He could only hear her deep breaths in the back seat. He was not sure if she was asleep. He thought of them, he thought of the last couple of days. It happened... All kinds of things happened, he did not want to think about it.

'Now it's all over.'

As they were coming out of the village, they sped past a shop in whose lit window there was a large photo of the president with the black crepe over it. He thought of Franjo Tuđman and felt a knot in his stomach. He was dead, definitely, now. They had kept him on life support for over a month, and then... who knew why, for some reason, on Saturday... it happened. He had had no time to think about this, about Tuđman, only when... If he hadn't died, he thought, they would've been in Zagreb yesterday, and by now they would've been sitting at home, him, Vanja... But he died. He was dead, laid out, people were coming to see him, the town was a nuthouse, the preparations, everything stopped, nothing worked, they couldn't have come, made arrangements...

'What about all the other people who died that day?' he asked himself. 'How did they...'

He heard a sigh coming from behind of his back and he stopped breathing. He felt the bitterness.

'And the two of us...'

They had neither parents nor an apartment...

'They thought we were going to the funeral.' He thought this was funny, disgusting.

The rain stopped and he turned off the wipers. For a while he had been driving through thick pine woods. He drove faster and faster and with more and more confidence, as if some invisible force had power over his body, and he did not resist it because he knew that everything was in vain, that everything was the way it was meant to be. He thought that there was no way out of this life and he got scared.

'Out!'

Everything was black! He needed a cigarette.

After a couple of kilometres, he saw a rest stop on his side of the road and he pulled over. All kinds of thoughts ran through his head. He stopped the car, opened the door quietly, and got out, without a jacket. Vanja was sleeping. It was cold, the air was sharp, and the sky was clear. The stars, like tiny pinheads, flickered above him. He took a deep breath, so deep that his lungs began to hurt. He took out a cigarette, but he did not light it. His body shivered. He approached the car and looked at her. She lay on the back seat all shrivelled, tiny, with her hands crossed over her chest. Her face was pale and her lips were tightly closed, as if she did not want to say a word even in her sleep.

'We did it. Because we had to.'

He thought...

As they had entered, they'd seen a short-haired pregnant woman sitting in the waiting room with a piercing in her nose, flipping through the newspapers. She'd smiled at them. The doctor had smiled as well, with the speakers releasing some relaxing music, they wanted to make it easier. But it didn't work. He wanted to kiss her, to hug her. That silence of hers. He could not remember when and why they...

He looked up into the sky. He waited for a star to fall, but it didn't. There were millions of stars, but as if out of spite, none of them moved. The only thing he saw was the fast, airy light of a satellite. He lit the cigarette. He remembered once, in winter, they were going home from Zagreb, it was night, it snowed, she was lying in the back seat, and he drove slowly, so that they wouldn't skid, so that they wouldn't slide away, and then at one moment, from somewhere in the woods, a deer ran out in front of him, a deer on the road covered with snow, he remembered, a deer, he asked himself which one of the two of them was going the wrong way, the woods glimmered, the moon, he cut the engine, watched the deer and it watched him back, it didn't move, and he, without taking his eyes off the road, quietly called Vanja to see it, to see how beautiful it was, how alive it was, but Vanja was asleep and he remembered that he had never loved anyone so much in his whole life, like then, like her while she was asleep, he remembered he loved her so much that he didn't want to wake her up, that he loved her so much that he let the deer run away, to escape her eyes, to preserve it for some other time, for now, for this kiss, for everything that was yet to happen.

Translated from the Croatian by Tomislav Kuzmanović

Contributors

Gyrðir Elíasson is one of Iceland's leading contemporary writers. His collection *Gula husid* (The Yellow House, 2000) received the Icelandic Literary Prize and The Halldor Laxness Literary Prize, and was nominated for the Nordic Council Literary Prize.

Frode Grytten was born in 1960 in Bergen, and grew up in Odda, a small industrial town on the Norwegian west coast. He is the author of a collection of poems *Start* (Start, 1983), two children's books, a travel book, and several short story collections: *Dans som en sommerfugl, stikk som en bie* (Dance Like a Butterfly, Sting Like a Bee, 1986), *Langdistansesvømmar* (Longdistanceswimmer, 1990), *80 grader aust for Birdland* (80 Degrees East of Birdland, 1993), *Meir enn regn* (More Than Rain, 1995), *Bikubesong* (Song of the Beehive, 1999), and *Popsongar* (Popsongs, 2001). His works have been translated into Swedish, Danish, Finnish, German, Dutch, Albanian, Croatian and Chinese.

Micheál Ó Conghaile was born in Galway in 1962. A prolific short story writer, playwright and novelist, Ó Conghaile has been a recipient of the Hennessy Literary Award, the Hennessy Young Irish Writer of the Year Award, and has been shortlisted for The *Irish Times* Literature Awards. His third collection of short stories, *An Fear nach nDéanann Gáire*, (The Man Who Never Laughs) was published in July 2003 to widespread acclaim. His work has been translated into Romanian, Croatian, Albanian, German and English.

Danielle Picard was a Professor of Classics, as well as a writer of short fiction. She died in 2004.

Mehmet Zaman Saçlıoğlu is one of Turkey's most prominent authors, most well known for his short stories. His collection *Summer House* received the Yunus Nadi Short Story Award in 1993, and the year after was awarded the Sait Falk Award, and a story from his second collection *Five Islands* won the Haldun Taner Short Story Prize. Some of his short stories have been translated into German and English. He lives in Istanbul and works in the Faculty of Fine Arts at Marmara University.

Ingo Schulze was born in Dresden in 1962 and studied classical philology at the University of Jena. He worked as the Director of the Altenburg Theater until 1990, and then became a newspaper editor, a job that took him to St. Petersburg for six months in 1993. Since then he has lived in Berlin. His first book, *33 Moments of Happiness* has won both the prestigious Doblin Prize and the Willner Prize for Literature. In 1998 his novel *Simple Stories* won the Berlin Literature Prize, and in 2007 his collection *Handy* won the Leipzig Book Fair Prize.

Roman Simić was born in 1972 in Zadar, Croatia. He is the Artistic Director for the Festival of the European Short Story and the editor of the series Anthologies of the European Short Story. His own short fiction has been included in various anthologies of contemporary Croatian prose and translated into many European languages. His publications include *U trenutku kao u divljini* (In the Moment Like in the Wilderness, 1996) which won the Goran prize for young poets; *Mjesto na kojem ćemo provesti noć* (A Place Where We're Going to Spend the Night, 2000), and *U što se zaljubljujemo* (What Are We Falling in Love With, 2005) which won the Jutarnji list prize for the best Croatian prose book of the year 2005, and is soon to be translated into German, Spanish, Slovenian and Serbian.

Jean Sprackland's first collection of poetry, *Tattoos for Mothers' Day* (Spike) was shortlisted for the Forward First Book Award and her second, *Hard Water* (Cape) is a Poetry Book Society Recommendation and was shortlisted for the 2003 T.S. Eliot Award. Her first sequence of short stories was published in *Ellipsis* (Comma, 2005). She lives in Southport.

Olga Tokarczuk is the author of several books of prose, including *Prawiek i inne czasy* (Prawiek and Other Times, 1996) and *Dom dzienny, dom nocny* (House of Day, House of Night, 1998). A number of her books have been translated from Polish to other languages, including French, German, Czech, Danish, Dutch, and Norwegian. Olga Tokarczuk lives in Nowa Ruda, Poland.

Mirja Unge was born in Stockholm in 1973. She received the Katapult Award for her critically acclaimed first novel, *Det var ur munnarna orden kom*, (It was from the mouths the words came, 1998). In 2000 she published her second novel, *Järnnätter* (Iron Nights). The same year her novel *Motsols* (Tide) was shortlisted for the Swedish Radio Award. In April 2007, her debut short story collection was published under the title *Brorsan är matt* (Brother is full) to widespread acclaim.

Special Thanks

This project has been realised only through the support and expertise of the following people: Helen Constantine and all at the Translators Association, Neasa Conroy, Roman Simic, Mirjana Cibulka, Amy Spangler, Lyn Marven, Antonia Lloyd-Jones, Vera Juliusdottir, Laura Pros Carey, Richard Crossan, Dave Eckersall, Kate Griffin, Natasha Periyan, Diana Reich, Will Carr, Sanja Maglov, Bruno Margitic, Marija Litovic, Tatjana Perusko, Gordana Matic, Snjezana Husic, Tomislav Brlek, Vedrana Berlengi, Stjepan Balent, Isabelle Croissant, Kate Griffin, and Matthew Crossan.

AVAILABLE FROM COMMA TRANSLATION...

Decapolis
Tales from Ten Cities

Ed. Maria Crossan

ISBN 9781905583034
RRP: £7.95

Featuring:
Larissa Boehning (Berlin), David Constantine (Manchester), Arnon Grunberg (Amsterdam), Emil Hakl (Prague), Amanda Michalopoulou (Athens), Empar Moliner (Barcelona), Aldo Nove (Milan), Jacques Réda (Paris), Dalibor Šimpraga (Zagreb), Ágúst Borgþór Sverrisson (Reykjavik).

Decapolis is a book which imagines the city otherwise. Bringing together ten writers from across Europe, it offers snapshots of their native cities, freezing for a moment the characters and complexities that define them. Ten cities: diverse, incompatible, contradictory – in everything from language to landscape.

'Europe is heavy with history and the trace left by cataclysm and upheaval. These are present in these tales, and yet coexist with a kind of wry and knowing playfulness.'
– A.S. Byatt in The Times

'The European short story is clearly in vigorous form.'
– Matthew Sweet, Nightwaves, Radio 3

'A fine, streetwise cacophony'
– The Independent

www.commapress.co.uk